She Wore A Badge

Deputy Marshal Mercer was a tough, no-nonsense badge-packer, and the tall, lean lawdog from El Paso was on the trail of three crazy convicts who'd just broken out of Huntsville Prison. When their trails finally crossed there was going to be bloodshed and gunsmoke and, for the killers, a surprise that might very well prove fatal, because Liberty Mercer was a woman.

But only a fool would underestimate Liberty. She was as handy with the Colt .45 at her hip as she was with the Winchester Model '86 she carried on her saddle. With a band of reinforcements in the shape of gunfighters Gabriel Moonlight, Latigo Rawlins, mysterious blind man Don Rojo and her father, the man they called Drifter, Liberty Mercer was primed and ready for the final showdown. . . .

She Wore A Badge

Steve Hayes

A Black Horse Western

ROBERT HALE · LONDON

ISBN 978-0-7198-0621-6

Robert Hale Limited
Clerkenwell House
Clerkenwell Green
London EC1R 0HT

www.halebooks.com

Typeset by
Derek Doyle & Associates, Shaw Heath
Printed and bound in Great Britain by
CPI Antony Rowe, Chippenham and Eastbourne

PREFACE

Enter the Museum of Art in downtown El Paso, Texas, and you will see two of my great-grandmother's paintings. They are on the east wall in the Western Studies section. One painting depicts an attractive, strong-featured woman in her mid-thirties with honest, gold-brown eyes and a splash of freckles across her farm-fresh face, sitting proudly astride a magnificent blue roan stallion. The background is typical of the sun-baked desert scrubland that still covers much of New Mexico and Texas today.

She is dressed mannishly for a woman in the late 1880s – jeans, plaid shirt, boots and a soiled campaign hat from under which poke wisps of sun-streaked brown hair. She's tall and lean and on her sun-faded blue denim jacket is pinned a Deputy US Marshal's star. She wears a holstered Colt .45 on her hip and there is a Winchester Model '86 in the saddle scabbard. The caption below the painting reads as follows: 'Lady Colt – Deputy US Marshal

Liberty Mercer – 1870-1957.'

The second painting depicts the same woman, only this time she is shooting it out with several tough gunmen in the middle of a dirt street in the dusty Mexican border town, Palomas. The caption below reads as follows: 'Lady Colt – Deputy US Marshal Liberty Mercer – 1870-1957.'

Because Liberty was a protégé of the legendary Texas lawman, US Marshal Ezra Macahan, these are two of the most popular paintings in the museum with adults and children alike. Most of them are familiar with her many arrests of gunmen and desperadoes, but few if any know much about her background – like the fact that she was expelled from St Mark's, a convent in Las Cruces, New Mexico, for 'conduct unbecoming a lady,' or that Liberty was not her birth name.

According to my great-grandmother, Hope, who, as a young girl was adopted by Liberty, she was born Emily Margaret Mercer. She changed her name to Liberty in homage to another Deputy US Marshal named Liberty who was shot in Mexico by the infamous gunman and bounty hunter, Latigo Rawlins – whom Liberty, as a teenager, almost married.

My great-grandmother often talked about writing a book about Liberty, but sadly died before she got around to it. Because of this, and because I feel the life of Lady Colt – as Liberty was nicknamed during her years as a Deputy US Marshal – is an important part of Texas history, I decided to take on the task.

I thought it would be easy. But I soon realized there was far more to Liberty's life than even my great-grandmother knew. Hence, what you read is derived from hand written records taken from the files of the US Marshal's office in El Paso; a personal diary in which Liberty wrote brief accounts of her cases; research material found in the library in Santa Rosa, NM, the town where Liberty was born and raised; and the sometimes far-fetched anecdotal tales my great-grandmother used to tell me whenever she came to visit my mother and grandma, who lived with us.

Enjoy.

NEW MEXICO

CHAPTER ONE

I came upon the horse first.

An old leggy blue roan stallion that had seen better days, it stood motionless beside the arroyo, saddle empty, reins hanging loose, a wild panicky look in its mottled gray-blue eyes as if it had been frightened by something.

I set my little sketchpad down next to my .22 single-shot, lever-action Ithaca and the ham sandwich I'd made before leaving home that morning, and eased my way through the brush toward it. I'm only ten, not yet tall enough to reach the jars of wild honey that Pa stores on the top shelf in our pantry, and I was toe-walking quiet as any Apache, but the stallion must have heard me because it snickered and nervously limped away from the wash.

That was when I realized its left foreleg was broken.

I also noticed there was blood on the saddle and on the stirrup facing me. I reckon I should have been scared; or if not scared, at least smart enough to hightail it home and tell Pa what I'd seen. But for some reason I wasn't scared – or smart – just curious, and I inched closer, softly clucking my tongue so the roan wouldn't get more spooked than it already was.

I was out of the brush and alongside a row of ocotillo bushes now. The stallion must have sensed I wasn't going to harm it because it stopped and stood there in the hot New Mexico sun, favoring its broken leg, eyeing me and breathing fast through its flared nostrils. Each time it breathed out foam sprayed over the bushes, covering them with white flecks, reminding me of when the cottonwoods are in bloom.

I inched closer. I could almost touch the roan now. It was trembling and its blotchy skin was twitching the same way horses twitch when it's hot and flies are bothering them. I talked softly to it, trying to soothe it and make it understand that I wasn't going to hurt it.

'Hold it . . . right there!'

The voice came from a clump of mesquite on my left, startling me.

'Don't move,' the voice said as I started to turn my head. 'I've got a bead on you. Try to run or pick up that rifle and I swear I'll drop you.'

I froze. I was truly scared now. I wished more than

9

anything that I'd run back home like I should have
done in the first place. Raising my hands above my
head, like the drunken rowdies do in town when
Sheriff McAllister arrests them, I tried to stop my
knees from knocking.

'Turn around . . . slowly . . . so's I can see your
face.'

'How can I turn around,' I said, 'if I'm not supposed to move?'

'Just do like I say.'

I turned.

'Why, you're only a young'un!'

The mesquite stirred and the woman stood up.
She was tall and lean and stood straight as a flagstick.
She wore a buckskin shirt, denim pants, black flat-
brimmed hat that hid most of her sun-streaked
brown hair and stirrup-worn cowhide boots. Her
empty holster was pegged down like a gunman. She
was old, but I reckon she was younger than Pa, who's
thirty and two. She was burned brown as me, and I'm
out in the sun all the time, and despite the trail dirt
on her face I knew most men would consider her
pretty.

'Stay right where you are,' she told me.

I obeyed and watched as she walked toward me.
She moved smooth and easy, like a bobcat on the
prowl. Because I want to be an artist, I try to notice
how folks look and move and what it is about them
that I'd remember if I were to draw them – and what
I remembered most about this woman was her eyes.

Wide-set and the color of molasses, they moved constantly, taking everything in, missing nothing, boring into me when they looked my way. It was unsettling; like being sized up by one of these gaunt Mexican wolves that come across the border now and then after a stray calf. The other thing I remembered about her was her expression. I could tell by the determined jut of her jaw and her tight-set lips that she was most likely as stubborn as me and would never back away from a fight. Lastly, I saw she was unarmed and realized she'd been running a bluff.

Neither of us spoke. She picked up my rifle and handed it to me, shaking her head as if embarrassed for mistaking me for an adult. 'Sorry I scared you, scout. But my horse threw me a-ways back and ran off. Been tracking it for hours. Then suddenly I saw you and. . . .' She paused, swaying as if feeling faint, and I thought she was going to fall.

But she didn't and I said: 'It's OK. I wasn't scared.'

I could tell she didn't believe me. Normally that wouldn't have bothered me. Lots of people don't believe me for various reasons and it's never bothered me before. But it did now and I felt disappointed in myself. First because I'd lied and gotten caught; and secondly, because although I didn't know this woman I wanted her to like me. I don't know why exactly. There was just something special about her, a quiet inner confidence that spilled out of her and for some reason made me feel confident too. I liked the feeling and not wanting her to think I was a liar, I was just about to admit that she had scared me when I noticed that her eyes had glazed over and she looked dizzy. But it only lasted a moment and then she became normal again.

'What're you doing here?' she asked.

'Drawing.'

'Drawing what?'

'Different things.'

'Like what?'

I picked up my little sketchpad and showed her the drawings I'd made on some of the pages. 'Anything that makes a good picture.'

'These are very good,' she said.

'Thank you.' I absently twisted one of my braids, a habit of mine when I'm nervous. 'See, I'm going to be an artist, a painter,' I said, hoping to impress her. 'Like Mr Remington.'

I could tell by the way her expression didn't change that she hadn't heard of Frederick Remington and I felt sorry for her ignorance. He can draw and paint horses better than any artist who ever lived and when I'm grown up I'm going to be just like him.

While I was thinking about Mr Remington the woman hunkered down beside the stallion and examined its broken foreleg. She cursed under her breath, like Pa does sometimes, but I could tell she was more sad than angry. If I could have painted her then I reckon she would have looked like the saddest person in the world. It seemed to me that she was hurting more than the horse. Rising, she pressed her cheek against its head, whispered something to it I couldn't hear, then stepped back and pulled her rifle from the scabbard under the saddle.

'Look away,' she told me. Waiting until I obeyed, she then shot the stallion. I jumped, startled, even though I knew what was going to happen, and heard the heavy thump as the horse collapsed on the ground.

'Sorry I had to do that in front of you,' she said. 'But he was in pain and I didn't want him to suffer.'

'It's all right. Pa had to shoot one of our horses last winter – a lineback called Ol' Charley. Stepped in a hole and broke its leg, just like your horse.' I paused and swallowed, hard, fighting down a lump that had pushed its way into my throat. 'I don't want you to think I get upset over every silly reason, but we'd had Ol' Charley a long time. Pa bought him from a trader just before Ma died in eighty-two and . . . and. . . .' I couldn't go on.

The woman nodded, as if understanding, and looked sadly at the dead blue roan. 'You'd never know it now, scout, but once *El Diablo* was the fastest, most beautiful stallion you ever saw.'

'I could tell that just by looking at him,' I said, trying to make her feel better. Then, as I thought about it: 'The Devil? That's a funny name for a horse.'

She didn't seem to hear me. She sighed and squeezed her brows together as if remembering something painful. 'I was only fourteen when Pa Mercer bought him. We've been together ever since – well, mostly. Other than when a bunch of Comancheros stole him along with our mares.'

'You all right?' I said as she swayed. 'You want to sit down or something?'

'Thanks, I'm fine.' She removed her hat, her long gold-brown hair spilling over her shoulders, and gingerly felt the back of her head. 'You live around here?'

I nodded. 'This wash marks the south side of our spread. All that mesquite strung out along there,' I pointed, 'that's the west boundary. And those rocks there and over there' – I thumbed at two rocky outcrops that looked skull-white in the noon sun – 'they make up the north and south boundaries.'

'In other words, I'm trespassing?'

'I never said that. Besides, Pa doesn't mind folks crossing our property – not so long as they're riding through.'

The woman lowered her hand and I saw blood on her fingertips.

'Goshawmighty, you're hurt!'

She nodded, looked vaguely at the blood and then collapsed.

Ma fainted once just before she passed, so I knew what to do next. I ran, fast as I could, to get Pa.

CHAPTER TWO

Pa and I quickly hitched up the team, jumped on the wagon, and raced back to the wash. But the woman was gone. Luckily for me, the blue roan still lay there dead or else I might have gotten a licking for making up stories. Pa's not quick to reach for his belt, but he truly hates liars.

The saddle was still on the stallion, which swarmed with flies, but the saddle-bags were gone. So was the Winchester '86 I'd seen tucked into the saddle boot. I figured the woman must have taken both with her. But I knew better than to waste time mentioning it to Pa, since he doesn't think much of my opinion anyhow. So I kept quiet and helped him get the saddle off the dead roan and into the wagon. Then, while he was examining the brand on the stallion's rump, I searched the area, hoping to find something that would tell me where the woman had gone. But all I found were a few blood spots on the sun-baked yellow dirt and an old tarnished Deputy US Marshal's star.

I showed it to Pa and asked him if I could keep it.

'Don't see why not,' he said. Typically, he didn't say anything else until we were halfway home in the wagon. Then he asked me if the woman had told me anything about herself.

'Nope.'

'Didn't say where she was from or what her name was?'

'Nope.'

Pa, not being much of a talker, didn't speak again until we'd reined up outside our barn and were unhitching the team. Then he said: 'You sure she didn't have no pistol?'

'Already told you I was. And it's didn't have *any* pistol,' I said, 'not *no* pistol.'

Pa hates it when I correct him. But he puts up with it because it's what Ma used to do all the time and he loves anything that reminds him of her.

'Then why do you think this woman's a gunman?' he asked.

'Already told you that, too.'

'Tell me again.'

'By the way she had her holster pegged down. You don't tie yours down and neither does anyone in town, except strangers riding through or coming up from the border – and most likely they're shootists or outlaws.'

Pa wasn't convinced. Like Ma used to say: 'It takes

a horse to kick him in the head to make him change his mind once it's made up.' And I could tell he'd made up his mind not to believe me.

'Well,' he said, chewing on each word, 'I been in a lot of towns from here to Texas and back, seen a lot of lawmen and hired guns, but so help me, Joshua, I ain't never seen no woman gunman. And I surely hope I never do.'

'So I'm making it all up, that what you're saying?'

'Uh-uh.' Pa scratched his curly red hair as if trying to figure out exactly what he was saying. He wasn't a tall man, at least not the kind who has to duck his head to enter a door, but he was big enough across the chest and shoulders for everyone to think he was a blacksmith. 'What I'm sayin', Hope, is it's peculiar is all. Mighty peculiar. I mean, how long you think a gunman's goin' to stay alive when he keeps losing his gun?'

'She,' I corrected, 'not he. And anyways, you don't know that she *keeps* losing it. For all you know this is the first time she's ever lost it. And maybe she wouldn't have lost it this time if her horse hadn't thrown her. And don't call me Hope,' I said crossly. 'You know I hate that name.'

'It's the name your ma give you,' Pa said, 'and out of respect for her, bless her loving soul, you'll use it long as I'm alive or face a whippin'. You follow?'

'Yes, sir,' I said, twisting my braids.

Pa frowned, a sure sign he was puzzled. 'Just don't fit,' he said like he was thinking aloud. 'If a horse threw you then ran off like she says hers did, and you saw your iron had fallen out of your holster, what's the first thing you'd do – pick it up, right?'

'Reckon.'

'Then how come she didn't?'

I shrugged. 'Maybe she couldn't find it?'

'Ha,' Pa snorted. 'I'll believe that when winter comes an' there ain't no frost.'

'*Isn't* any frost,' I corrected. Then as he scowled: 'Believe what you want. It doesn't make any differ-ence to me. I know what I saw and nobody can tell me different. Not even you.' I looked off at the trail that led out across the flat, sun-scorched scrubland to town and saw something that made me smile. 'Tell you what,' I added, 'if you don't believe me, you can ask her yourself.'

'How am I supposed to do that when I don't where she is?'

'Just sit a spell.' I thumbed toward the trail. 'Few minutes, she'll be standing in front of you.' I left him gaping and led the team into the barn.

Once I'd put the horses into their stalls and grained them, I stood by the half-open door ready to listen to Pa and the woman talking. Reason I did this, and didn't go out and join him, is he thinks young'uns shouldn't be around or even listening when grown-ups are talking; and if I'd come out of the barn he would have right off told me to go fix supper.

The woman, who was almost as tall as Pa, got

within a few steps of him then staggered, dropped her rifle and saddle-bags and collapsed.

Pa knelt beside her, scooped her up like she weighed nothing and carried her indoors.

Knowing he'd need my help, I left the barn and ran to the house.

CHAPTER THREE

Pa heard me come running in. He'd just finished setting the woman down on the bed in my room and without looking back, through the doorway, he told me to bring him some cold water and a towel – '*Pronto*!'

I obeyed, fast as I could, and tried not to spill the water as I carried Ma's favorite porcelain basin from the sink to the bed. 'She all right?' I asked as he dipped the towel into the water and wrung it out before gently bathing the woman's face. 'I mean, she's not going to die, is she?'

Pa ignored me, like always. Wetting and wringing out the towel again, he folded it and placed it on the woman's forehead. 'Whiskey,' he said.

I ran out.

Pa kept the whiskey on the same shelf as the wild honey. I dragged a chair into the pantry, stood on it and carefully took down the jug. On my way back to the bedroom I grabbed a mug from the kitchen shelf, figuring that it'd be easier to drink from than the jug.

If Pa thought I'd used my head for once, like he's always telling me to, he didn't mention it. Removing the cork with his teeth he poured a little whiskey into the mug, handed me back the jug and then held the mug to the woman's chapped lips. Her eyelids fluttered. But she didn't drink. Pa put his hand under her head and raised it, at the same time prying her lips open with the rim of the mug. A trickle of whiskey entered her mouth. The woman stirred, sighed, opened her eyes and blinked owlishly around as she tried to figure out where she was.

'Drink,' Pa said. He tilted the mug to make it easier for her. 'Make you feel better.'

She drank a few sips and then looked questioningly at Pa.

'We'll talk later,' he promised. 'First, we got to tend to that cut on your head.' To me he added: 'Fetch me the iodine and that ol' white shirt you're always grumbling 'bout havin' to sew. *Pronto!*'

I did as I was told. Pa's right. I do grumble when he asks me to sew on a button or stitch up a tear on his white cotton shirt. But that's only because the shirt is really old and has been patched more times than I can remember. Truth is, if it was any other shirt he would've burned it long ago. But Ma bought him the shirt about six months before she passed and just seeing it reminds him of her. It's the same way I feel about the paints she bought me after she came back from the doctor in Las Cruces, so I reckon I shouldn't grumble.

When I returned beside the bed the woman was lying on her side, her back to Pa, and he was dabbing iodine on an ugly gash behind her right ear. Iodine stings worse than anything. I know. Pa loves to pour it on my knees or elbows if I fall and scrape the skin. But unlike me, the woman didn't flinch or cry or yell at Pa to stop. She just waited till he was finished and had torn off one of the sleeves of his shirt, ripped it in half and used it to bandage her head, then she rolled over, sat up and thanked him.

It was right then that I started to admire her.

Pa, being Pa, didn't say much. He listened as she said her name was Liberty Mercer and that she was a Deputy US Marshal out of El Paso.

Pa scratched his curly red hair. 'You've come a far piece.'

'Far enough.'

She wasn't one to waste words. I could tell Pa liked that about her. He scratched his hair again, a sure sign he was puzzled by the fact that she wasn't trying to talk his ear off, like most of the widows in town do when they stop him on the street.

'How come you ain't wearin' a star?' he asked her.

'I lost it while I was trying to run down my horse.'

'Uh-huh,' Pa said. He stuck his hand out to me. I grudgingly dug the old star out of my pocket and gave it to him. 'This it?' he asked Liberty.

'Why, yes!' Then to me: 'Where'd you find it?'

I explained.

'She didn't find your pistol, though,' Pa said, sounding suspicious. 'Reckon you must've lost that afore – maybe when you was throwed?'

Liberty nodded, wincing as she did, and gingerly touched the back of her head.

'Don't do that,' Pa told her. 'You'll infect it.'

Liberty took her hand away. She had fine strong hands with long slender fingers like Miss Deacon, who plays the organ in church on Sundays, and a graceful way of moving them that reminded me of my mother. The way she spoke reminded me of Ma, too, and I couldn't help wondering why such a cultured woman would want to become a lawman.

Pa said, in that blunt way of his: 'What made your horse throw you?'

'A rattler spooked it,' Liberty said. 'He was getting up in years and he didn't see it until the last minute. Caught us both by surprise and I fell off and hit my head on a rock and blacked out. When I came around I was already on my feet and had walked a-ways. I tried to find my way back to the rocks, but you know how it is – everything looks the same and I figured I'd be better off finding my horse first.' She closed her eyes, dizzy for a moment, then said to me: 'I'm obliged to you. That star means an awful lot to me.'

'Just an old scratched-up badge.'

'It's much more than that, believe me. Belonged to someone I cared about and admired, another deputy who was shot in Mexico by one of the convicts

I'm after now.'

'You're tracking escaped convicts?' I said, awed.

'Hush,' Pa said. 'Mind your business, girl, an' go fix supper.'

For once I was too excited to obey him. 'How many of them are there?' I asked Liberty.

'Three. They broke out of Huntsville Prison last month.'

'What makes you think they're around here?' Pa said.

'They were seen by a constable in El Paso a few days ago. They shot his horse out from under him and killed his partner. Then yesterday I got a wire from the sheriff in Santa Rosa – said three men fitting their description shot a rancher between here and the border, stole his stock and, according to his neighbor, who talked to him later, then rode off in this direction.'

'What's his name?' Pa said. 'The rancher, I mean?'

'Whitlock. You know him?'

'Sure we do,' I said. 'I painted a picture of his dog last fall.'

'Is Henry dead?' asked Pa.

'No. But according to Sheriff McAllister he's shot up pretty badly.' To me she said: 'Listen, can you take me back to where I first saw you?'

'Sure. It's not far. Why?'

'Like this star, the gun means a lot to me.'

'It isn't there. I already looked.' Seeing how disappointed she was, I said: 'But maybe if you described the place where your horse got spooked, I could take you there and help you look for your gun.'

'Would that be all right with you, Mr—?'

'Corrigan,' Pa said. 'Lyle Corrigan.' He shrugged, adding: 'Reckon. But you ain't goin' no place right now, ma'am. Not unless you want to fall out of the saddle 'fore you clear my property.'

'But—'

Pa stopped her. 'No point in arguin',' he said firmly. 'You need rest and food. You'll stay here tonight. My daughter can sleep in the barn.'

'No,' Liberty said. 'She shouldn't have to give up her bed. I'll be happy to sleep in the barn.'

Pa wasn't listening, like always. To me he said, 'I won't ask you again to fix supper,' and walked out, carrying the basin of water with him.

'I better do as he says,' I told Liberty. 'Then tomorrow we can start first light. Pa's got your saddle. You can use his horse. He won't mind.' I hurried out before she could argue.

CHAPTER FOUR

It wasn't a hardship for me to sleep in the barn. Truth is I liked it. Sleeping by myself under a blanket on the loose hay we keep stored in the loft above the horses made me feel like I was grown up.

I even made a game out of it. Just before falling asleep I pretended I was this famous artist, snuggled up in my bedroll under the stars, smoking a hand-rolled as I figured out from what perspective I was going to paint *Dos Hombres*, two towering, human-shaped rocky bluffs overlooking the south boundary of what used to be the Double C spread.

Once owned by a tough, mean-spirited old cattle-man named Stillman J. Stadtlander, it had been the biggest ranch in the whole territory. But when he died a few years back and there wasn't any family still alive to leave it to, the lawyers moved in. They split the land into sections that Pa says were sold off to a bunch of different businessmen. Easterners. The first thing they did was fence off all their property so that now you can't ride from sunrise to sunset, but have to get permission from the foreman of each ranch just to cross their land. Pa calls it progress, whatever that means, but all I know is it's getting so you might as well live in a city for all the open range and freedom to ride it you got left nowadays. I don't know any of the foremen, which is why it's important I know from what angle I want to paint the bluffs before I go dragging my easel and paints around and getting permission from the wrong ramrod.

I was still thinking about that when I fell asleep. Next thing I knew I was opening my eyes. It was dawn and through a crack in the planking I could see the clouds turning pink along the edges as the sun came up.

It was time to fire up the stove and start breakfast. Pulling on my jeans and boots, I buttoned up my shirt, shinned down the ladder to the floor and ran outside. Above the mountains to the east it looked like God had set the sky on fire. If I'd had time I would have set up the easel Pa made me and painted a real fine picture. But a promise is a promise and daylight wasn't far off, so I hurried indoors.

The sight of the coffee pot already atop the stove and Pa cracking eggs into a skillet like he knew how to cook stopped me short. 'W-What're you doin'?' I said, surprised.

'Fixin' breakfast, what's it look like?' he said gruffly. He made it sound like it was something he did every morning and I was so flummoxed I didn't have any comeback. 'Well, don't just stand there,' he added, 'set the table like your ma used to.'

' 'Mean, with a *tablecloth*?'

'And the good china,' Pa said. 'An' mind your manners when you eat.'

'Yes, sir,' I said. Entering the bedroom, I kneeled before Ma's hope chest, as she called it, a large trunk that was kept at the foot of the bed, and opened the lid. The smell of camphor tickled my nose. I remembered when I was little asking Ma what all the tiny white balls were for and her smiling so that her dimples showed and the corners of her big, china-blue eyes crinkled, saying, voice gentle as spring rain: 'Why, to keep the moths away, dearest.'

Now as I took out the carefully folded, snowy Irish linen tablecloth and napkins I heard her voice again. It was as clear as if she was right beside me, and without thinking I turned and was surprised not to see her standing there. My eyes watered. I fisted the tears away, angry at myself for acting like a lost calf. Putting the tablecloth aside I began removing the dishes and cups and knives and forks and spoons that even when Ma was alive we never used except on Sundays or when neighbors came to supper … or to listen to Ma sing.

She had a fine clear voice and was never off key, like the Widow Hadley who sings on Sunday morning at church. Sometimes when Pa listened to her he would get tears in his eyes and after everyone had left

28

I'd hear him in the bedroom telling Ma how proud he was just to be her husband.

I was proud of her, too. And more than anything, I wanted her to be proud of me – which is why I practised so hard to speak correctly, like she always wanted me to.

Pa seemed to enjoy eating breakfast with Liberty. Once, he actually laughed at something she said. It wasn't one of those loud, knee-slapping laughs, the way he used to laugh when Ma was alive, but it was definitely a laugh and he was definitely happy for those few moments – happier than I'd ever seen him since that Sunday morning when he found Ma lying face-down in the barn, one hand still clasping the handle of the egg-basket, the other bent under her as if she'd tried to break her fall.

Knowing he was happy made me happy. And, *loco* as it sounds, for a moment I wondered how it would be to have Liberty for a mother. I watched her as she ate and talked to Pa and though she wasn't as beautiful as Ma, and most likely not as kind or gentle, she was very nice and by the time breakfast was done and she'd finished helping me with the dishes, I liked her a lot and figured Pa and I could do much worse than having her with us all the time. 'Course, that wasn't going to happen, even at my age I knew that, but I saw no harm in thinking about it. Strangely, at the same time I couldn't help feeling sad for Pa, who, no matter how hard I tried to make him happy, never was and instead seemed to have lost all interest in life – as well as me, most likely – and was just waiting to die so he could be with Ma again.

CHAPTER FIVE

Because of all the painting I do outdoors, I reckon I know the land for miles around as well as any hawk or jackrabbit. Painting something, no matter if it's a cactus, wild flower or distant mountains makes me remember it and where it was – which is I why I had no trouble finding the place where Liberty's horse got spooked and threw her once she described it to me.

It was a little more than an hour's ride southwest from our spread: a canyon filled with rocks and gullies and sidewinders, flanked on both sides by smooth, round, ochre- and peach-colored hills. Liberty recognized the canyon as soon as we entered it. She rode the bay Pa had loaned her on ahead of me, head down, scanning the rocks and the hard yellow dirt for any sign of her gun. She said it was a Colt .45 with cedar grips, and after a little I veered off to search among the rocks on the opposite side of the canyon.

'Look out for rattlers,' she warned me.

Inside, I smiled to myself. Years of suddenly hearing that deadly whirring rattle as I traipsed about looking for things to paint had put me on constant alert and now it was almost second nature to me. But it was kind of her to worry about me and again it made me realize how nice it would be for Pa, and for me, to wake up and know that Liberty was part of our family.

We must've searched for an hour or more and were nearly at the other end of the canyon when Liberty gave a shout and called out to me. 'Over here! Look! I've found it, Hope! I've found it!'

I looked up and saw her waving the six-gun at me. We were both on foot now and I ran, whooping over the rocks to her. She holstered the Colt and held out her arms to me. Without thinking I jumped into them and we hugged so hard both of us lost our balance and almost fell over.

It was one of the best feelings I've ever had – and easily the best since Ma passed.

'That's twice you've brought me luck,' she exclaimed. She joyfully swung me around and then set me down and we stood there in the hot sun laughing and giggling with me hopping around and whooping like a drunken Apache.

'I don't know how I'm ever going to thank you, scout.'

'Nothing to thank me for. You found it, not me.'

'Yes, but you're the one who led me here. Without

you, scout, I would have lost one of the things I cherish most.'

As she stared lovingly at the big Colt, feeling happy for her, I said: 'This deputy who gave the gun – why'd you like her so much?'

Liberty looked up and stared off, her lidded gold-brown eyes seeing something only she saw, her tanned, freckle-nosed face as sad as Pa's when he's putting flowers on Ma's grave.

'It's hard to describe,' she said distantly. 'I mean, we didn't know each other for very long, and yet in those few days she ... we seemed to understand everything about each other. You know. How we felt . . . the thoughts we were thinking . . . things we both believed in . . . it was like we'd known each other all our lives.' She paused, frowning for a moment, before saying: 'Funny thing is, scout, in many other ways, how we were raised . . . taught to think . . . our schooling, couldn't have been more different. Liberty was an orphan and I—'

'Liberty,' I said surprised. 'Her name was Liberty, too?'

'Uh-huh.'

'Liberty what?'

'Just Liberty. Said this madam who helped raise her in Oklahoma called her that because it's what her boy died for during the Civil War.'

' 'Mean it wasn't her real name?'

'Wasn't her birth name, if that's what you mean, no. But then it isn't mine, either. I was born Emily

Margaret Mercer.'

I was pure gaggle-confused. 'Then why d'you call yourself Liberty?'

'Because of her. How much she meant to me . . . meant to all women who feel there is more to life than just sitting at home sewing, knitting or having babies. Liberty was one of the very first US Deputy Marshals ever sworn in, which paved the way for the rest of us. What's more, she had to go through all kinds of hell and insults, not to mention years of waiting around, filing papers while being passed over for men who weren't as capable as she was before one day, she was finally sworn in by a marshal who believed in her. And then,' Liberty said with a disgusted snort, 'wouldn't you know it? Just as she started to make a fine reputation for herself, she gets herself killed, shot down without a chance by a gunman hiding in a house in Mexico.'

'Is that why you're hunting him?' I said, 'so you can pay him back for killing your friend?'

'That's one of the reasons, yes.'

'What're the others?'

'They're murderers, all three of them.'

'Any other reason?'

'Why do you ask?'

'No reason.'

Liberty looked at me. Her eyes pierced me like arrows. Though she didn't say anything I felt as if I'd been scolded for lying – again.

'I just wanted to know,' I said lamely. 'I'm not

trying to be nosy or anything, like Pa thinks, I just get curious – 'specially when I meet someone new. I want to know all about them.'

Liberty nodded slowly, as if accepting my explanation.

'You're not mad at me, are you?' I said.

She smiled, ''Course not.' She unscrewed the cap of her canteen, took a gulp and then offered it to me. 'Well, all I can say is, like I told you and your father, they're escaped convicts and it's my job to catch them and bring them to justice. Is that reason enough?'

I nodded. But much as I trusted her, I still sensed there was something more; some other reason that she was not sharing with me that was driving her to catch these outlaws. But I couldn't think of what it could be and, as Pa has drummed into me, it's not polite to keep asking folks you barely know questions. So I swallowed some water, felt it go down lukewarm and penny-tasting, and handed back the canteen.

'We best be getting back,' I said. 'Pa gets all upset if I'm gone too long.'

Liberty nodded, as if understanding that I had things on my mind, too, and then did something I wasn't expecting: she hunkered down so that her face was level with mine and I could see deep into her gold-brown eyes. Then said gently: 'After you get back home, we probably won't ever see each other again, scout. So I want to tell you something now. I've known a lot of girls – some younger, some your age or older, either at the convent or in towns all across Texas and here in New Mexico – and none of them, not a single one, was as special as you. Always keep that in mind, OK?'

I didn't know what to say so I nodded.

'And if there's ever a time when you need help of any kind, I want you to remember me as your friend – someone you can trust and rely on to makes things right. Will you do that?'

I nodded again; again not sure what to say.

'Good. You can always reach me by wire or letter, care of my name at the marshal's office in El Paso.' She hugged me, her cheek hot against mine, and though I wasn't sure what had brought all this affection on, I had to admit it felt warm and comforting and I knew I had a friend for life.

CHAPTER SIX

We were riding up out of a little gully, less than a pistol shot from the house, when I first saw the piebald tied up to the front porch. Liberty saw it about the same time and, reining up, asked me if I knew who it belonged to.

'Sure,' I said. 'Sheriff McAllister.'

'Curt McAllister?'

'Uh-huh. You know him?'

'No. But soon as I heard those three convicts were headed this way I wired Sheriff McAllister, describing them and warning him to be on the lookout.'

'That's most likely why he's here, then,' I said as we rode on, 'to warn Pa and me about them.'

As we rode up, Sheriff McAllister must have heard us coming because he came out of the house and stood watching us from the porch. He and my father are pals, even though they always argue when they play checkers, and I wondered where Pa was and why he hadn't come out with the sheriff. I also wondered why the sheriff wasn't smiling, like he usually does when he sees me, and figured it was probably because he was worried about the escaped convicts.

Reining up in front of the porch I started to greet him. But he stopped me by raising his hand. Then, stepping off the porch, he grasped the bridle of my horse and squinting up at me from under the brim of his dark gray hat, said grimly: 'Don't get down, Miss Hope.'

'Why not?'

' 'Cause I say so,' he said, firmly but not unkindly.

Now Sheriff McAllister is a tall drink of water, and quiet mostly, but like everyone in Santa Rosa says, there's something about him – way he looks at you with his steely gray eyes and tight white lips – that makes you pay attention to what he says.

So I stayed put in the saddle. But I couldn't help wondering why he wasn't calling me Cricket, as he usually does, and, curious, I said: 'Where's Pa?'

'We'll get to that later,' he promised. Then to Liberty: 'Reckon you'd be Deputy Mercer.'

Liberty nodded. 'And you're Sheriff McAllister?' When he nodded, she added: 'Any reason I can't step down?'

'Go ahead,' he told her. 'But I'd be much 'bliged if you'd go into the house and wait there for me. Miss Hope an' me, we got some talkin' to do.'

'Sure thing,' Liberty said.

Sheriff McAllister waited until she had gone inside and then smiled at me with the saddest eyes I've ever seen. Then he reached up, 'You can get down now,' he said, and helped me slide down from the saddle.

For some strange reason I started to get worried. 'Is something wrong, Sheriff? Has something happened to Pa?'

He took a deep breath and let it out slowly, so that under his iron-gray mustache his upper lip fluttered. 'How long you knowed me, Cricket?'

'Since I was born almost. Why?'

'In all that time I ever lied to you, or treated you bad?'

'No, sir. Not me or Pa.'

'An' you know I'd never do nothin' to hurt you?'

' 'Course not.'

That seemed to please him. Hunkering down in front of me, he pushed his hat back a little so I could see his whole face, the sadness in it, and then he gently grasped me by both shoulders and said, his deep voice raspier than I've ever heard it: 'Your Pa . . . he's . . dead, Cricket.'

I heard him all right – the words, but I wouldn't believe him. 'W-what do you mean?'

'Somebody killed him—'

'No!' I said, my legs buckling. 'No-you're-lying-he-can't-be-dead!'

'Only wish that was true, but—'

'No! No! Not Pa! H-He can't be he can't be he can't—!'

I tried to run but Sheriff McAllister's big hands gripped my shoulders even harder, stopping me, holding me there, keeping me right in front of him, even though I struggled and screamed and tried break loose.

Then, gradually, like when the sky gets all dark and there's thunder and lightning and hard as you try you can't pretend any more that a storm isn't coming, I realized it was true: Pa really was dead – like Ma – and all the fight went out of me and I stopped struggling and started sobbing and all this time my legs were buckling and I would have fallen if the sheriff hadn't wrapped his long arms around me and pulled me close, squeezing me hard like my mother did the night before her heart gave out.

Then everything went quiet.

Dark.

CHAPTER SEVEN

The next thing I remember is opening my eyes and looking around, trying to figure out where I was. At first nothing looked familiar. Then, slowly, I began to recognize things; furniture, cabinets, pictures I'd seen before – everything coming back to me now, clear as Deer Creek after a rain, water so sparkling clean that below the surface you can see the trout hovering, perfectly still, eyes upturned as they watch for insects, their slim shadows darkening the white pebbles at the bottom – and realized, with something of a shock, that I wasn't home anymore but lying on a table in Dr Jacobs's dark little office.

'Well, now, missy, decided to wake up, did you?'

Dr Jacobs' red, fleshy, smiling face leaned over me.

'We were starting to get worried about you.'

I looked at him – at his dark friendly eyes, huge behind his thick spectacles – without saying anything. I like Dr Jacobs. Everybody does. Even folks who hate Jews. Pa says it's because he treats everyone

41

fairly and never complains when they don't pay their bills. I don't know if that's true, or care much either – I like him because of the kind, gentle way he cared for Ma when she got sick once when Pa thought she had the fever.

'W-Why am I here?' I heard myself ask.

Liberty's face appeared next to the doctor's. Her hat was off, her hair hanging down like sunshine, and she looked worried and relieved at the same time. 'You passed out, scout. The sheriff and I figured the doctor ought to take a look at you – make sure you were all right – so we brought you here. How're you feeling?'

'OK, I reckon. . . . Where's Pa?'

Liberty and the doctor exchanged looks, like grown-ups always do when they don't want to tell you something bad.

'We can talk about that later,' Dr Jacobs said, smiling his doctor's smile. 'Right now, young lady, you need to let me examine you—'

'He's dead, isn't he?' I said, remembering.

Liberty nodded. 'I'm awfully sorry, scout.'

There was a roaring in my ears. I sat up. The room spun. I felt dizzy. I blinked a few times. The room slowly stopped spinning. But not the roaring.

'Better lie down,' Dr Jacobs said. 'You've had a nasty shock and—'

'How?' I said, pushing his hands away. 'Who did it?'

'Not sure yet,' Liberty said, 'but I figure it's got to

be the three men I'm after.'

'Why? They don't know Pa, do they?'

'Wouldn't matter. Not to these men. They're born killers. Not even fit for wolf-bait. 'Specially Canfield and Dano. Robbing, raping, killing – means nothing to them. They want something, they take it.'

' 'Mean, like our stock?'

'Stock . . . food . . . gold—'

'We don't have any gold. Pa would've told 'em that.'

'I'm sure he did. But they probably didn't believe him. Figured he was lying – that he'd squirreled it away somewhere – and tried to force him to tell them where.'

'So they shot him?'

Liberty hesitated.

'Please . . . I have to know.'

She nodded, understanding. 'Mostly, they used their fists.'

I felt sick. Knowing how stubborn Pa is, I knew he must have suffered a lot before he died.

'You saw him? His body, I mean?'

She nodded. I could tell by her eyes and the grim, tight set of her mouth that what she'd seen she didn't want to talk about.

'I want to see him,' I said.

'Sure, sure,' Dr Jacobs said. 'You will. In time. But not right now.'

I ignored him and looked at Liberty. 'It's my right, you know. He's – was my father. All I got.'

43

'I know that,' Liberty said. She seemed to be hurting as much as I was. 'And if that's what you really want, I'll take you to him.'

'Marshal,' began Dr Jacobs.

She silenced him with a look. To me she said: 'You trust me, don't you?'

I nodded.

'Then you know I wouldn't say something unless it was true.'

I nodded again.

'Well, the truth is, might be better all around if you waited a little before you saw your Pa. Dying changes the way people look. And it isn't always for the best. So if it was me, I'd give the undertaker time to make my father look more like I remembered him.'

I twisted one of my braids. 'You promise I'll get to see him before they . . . you know . . . put him next to Ma?'

'Got my word on it.'

'All right,' I said grudgingly. 'I'll wait.'

Liberty smiled that make-you-feel-good smile of hers, and beside her Dr Jacobs sighed with relief.

'If you're hungry, I'll take you somewhere to get something to eat.'

I wasn't hungry. I wasn't anything. I couldn't even cry.

But I did want to be with Liberty.

'I could drink a glass of lemonade,' I said. 'I'm right thirsty.'

'Lemonade it is,' Liberty said. She helped me down off the table. 'Just tell me where your favorite place is and we'll go there.'

But we never got to drink lemonade. We'd no sooner left the doctor's office and were about to cross the street to Rose's Café when Sheriff McAllister came hurrying up to Liberty.

'Just came in,' he said, handing her a wire. 'From the El Paso office.'

Liberty read the wire to herself first; then aloud to the sheriff.

'HUNTSVILLE WARDEN SAYS RAWLINS TOLD CELLMATE IF HE MADE IT OUT HE PLANNED TO HOLE UP IN CHIHUAHUA AT MESQUITE STOP NO ONE HERES HEARD OF TOWN STOP ASK AROUND STOP MAYBE SHERIFF OR SOMEONE IN SANTA ROSA KNOWS WHERE IT IS.'

'Not me,' Sheriff McAllister said as Liberty looked up from the wire.

'But I wasn't born an' raised here, like some folks. Now Frank, over at the barbershop, I reckon he'd know where it is if anyone would.'

'It's not a town,' Liberty said with an odd smile. 'It's a person.'

'A person – how do you mean?'

'Ever hear of the outlaw Mesquite Jennings?'

'Nope. Can't say as I have.'

I hadn't either, but I didn't say anything.

'He and Rawlins are old friends – used to ride

45

together a long time ago. They and two others: Ben Lawless and his cousin, Will. They were all in their twenties then and wild as Apaches, and I remember Gabe saying—'

'Gabe?'

'Gabriel Moonlight – that's his real name. Mesquite Jennings was an alias. Anyway, I remember Gabe telling my father – who also knew him – that he and Rawlins were there, in Mexico, when Ben and Will shot it out and Ben was killed—'

'By his own cousin?'

'According to Gabe, yes. Made Rawlins so angry he forced Will to draw and gunned him down.'

'Huh,' the sheriff said. He scratched his stubbly chin. 'Sounds like a right friendly bunch.'

There was silence save for the rattle and creak and jingle made by wagons, buckboards and riders passing behind us.

I know it's rude to ask questions but I had to know something. 'Your Pa – is – was he an outlaw too?'

Liberty smiled. 'No. He's a wrangler – or was when I was your age. Now he raises horses on this ranch we bought just outside El Paso. Not the most exciting life,' she admitted, 'especially when I'm gone. But my father seems to have adjusted to it. Or so he says.' To Sheriff McAllister she added: 'I'll be leaving right after the funeral tomorrow.'

'Goin' after Rawlins an' the others, are you?'

Liberty nodded.

The sheriff frowned, concerned. 'Maybe you

46

ought to think twice 'bout that, Deputy.'

'Why's that?'

'Your star ain't gonna mean squat once you cross the border.'

'I won't be wearing it,' Liberty said. 'This is personal.'

CHAPTER EIGHT

Pa's younger brother, Delvin, had a chicken ranch just north of the border. Years ago he and Pa came out from St Jo' together and from what Ma told me, they were always real close. But that all ended last spring when Uncle Del, as I call him, went to Deming to buy a prize rooster and instead come back with a pretty new wife on his arm. She's Mexican, but speaks English better than I do, and Pa says she can't be more than eighteen. Her name's Consuelo, though everyone calls her Connie, and I like her a lot because she acts more like my sister than my aunt.

But Pa, he hates her so much he stopped talking to Uncle Del entirely. Worse, he won't let me go visit them at their ranch or speak to either of them, not even if I bump into them in Santa Rosa. I asked him once why he hated Aunt Connie like he did and he just grunted and told me it wasn't any of my business. But one night when Sheriff McAllister came over for supper and to play checkers, I heard them talking

48

about Aunt Connie. I wasn't supposed to be listening, but I left my bedroom door open and heard Pa
saying how she used to be a whore in the *El Tecolote*
cantina in Palomas, which is a little *pueblo* 'cross the
border from Columbus full of outlaws and border
trash, whatever that means. I wondered what Pa was
doing in the cantina in the first place, and in the
second place how he knew Aunt Connie was a whore
if, like he's always told me, he's never had any deal-
ings with whores. But naturally I never got around to
asking him.

Anyways, reason I brought this up is that Sheriff
McAllister says that now Pa is dead, I have to go live
with Uncle Del and Aunt Connie because they're my
only living relatives. He, Liberty and I were eating
supper in Rose's Café when he told me this and I
reckoned, 'cause of my age, I didn't have any choice
but to do as he said. But I figured I did have a right
to know when I was going there, and who was going
to take me, so I asked him.

'Depends,' he said.

'On what?'

'If your Uncle Del or Aunt Connie come to the
funeral tomorrow.'

'Why would they do that?' I said. 'They most likely
don't even know Pa's dead.'

'Sure they do.' Sheriff McAllister chased some
peas around his plate with a fork and shoveled them
into his mouth before adding: 'My deputy, Tom
Meeks, had to ride over to Columbus to pick up a

prisoner, an' since it wasn't much out of his way I told him to stop an' give your uncle the news. 'Course, Del an' your pa feelin' the way they did 'bout each other, he might not show up at the funeral. An' if that happens, then I'll take you over there myself. How's that sound, Miss Hope?'

I shrugged, knowing my opinion didn't really count anyways. 'What about where I am now?' I asked. 'Why can't I just go on living there? It's mine, isn't it, now Pa's gone? I mean, I know I'm only ten but Pa taught me what to do, what's got to be done every day to keep things running, and it's not as if we got Apaches or Comanches raiding us anymore, so—'

The sheriff held up his tanned, thick-fingered hand, silencing me. 'Indians or no Indians,' he said firmly, 'you can't run that spread alone. You can't live there alone, neither. We might be headed into the next century, like all the politicians an' progress folks keep remindin' us, but this territory's still wild enough to keep me an' the marshal, here, in business. Ain't that right, ma'am?' he added to Liberty.

She nodded and smiled at me. She had beautiful straight teeth that were whiter than the plate I was eating off, and I told myself if I ever painted her I'd make sure she was smiling. 'Sheriff's right, scout. If he wasn't, I'd be back in El Paso, helping my father raise horses instead of chasing after escaped cons and murderers.' She pressed her cool hand over mine and squeezed fondly. 'Just imagine what they'd do to you if they happened to show up at your place?'

' 'Sides,' Sheriff McAllister added, 'you like your Uncle Del and Aunt Connie – you've told me so yourself, many times, remember?'

'Sure,' I said. 'I like them. Like them lots. But that doesn't mean I want to go live with them – them or their dumb old chickens.'

Of course, what I wanted or didn't want didn't really matter a lick. It never has, not since Ma passed. She was the only one who ever listened to me when I complained or thought I was right about something – what's more, she stuck up for me and believed in me, and my future as an artist, and actually told Pa on two occasions that even though I was only knee-high to a gnat, I still had a right to have an opinion!

Now, as we finished supper, and the three of us crossed the street to the Carlisle Hotel where I was going to spend the night in Liberty's room, at her insistence so I wouldn't be all alone on the day my father died, I thought about how my life had changed since my mother passed; and how, now with Pa gone, it was going to change again, and how both times I was unable to stop that change or even have any say in the matter – not even though it was my life, my future that other folks were deciding for me.

That night in the hotel room I lay there in bed in the dark, staring up at the ceiling and listening to the mariachi band playing across the street in Rosario's Cantina. The sound of the music hid all the other sounds going on in the street and I was glad I had something to listen to because it kept my mind off Pa dying and the funeral tomorrow. I still hadn't cried yet and I kept wondering what was wrong with me, because when Ma died I cried and kept crying off and on for days, weeks even.

I must have been thinking out loud without realizing it 'cause Liberty, who was lying next to me, suddenly sat up, clasped her hands around her knees and asked me what was wrong.

'Nothing,' I said.

'If you'd like to talk to me, about anything,' she said, 'I'd be happy to listen. That's OK,' she added when I didn't answer, 'I didn't want to talk to anyone either when someone I loved died.'

'Who was it?' I asked, curious.

It was then she told me about how when she was sixteen and going to school at a convent in Las Cruces, Comancheros had raided the ranch she grew up on, killing what she'd thought then was her whole family and stealing all their horses. She added that it wasn't until she came home for the funeral that she discovered a man known as Drifter, a wrangler who used to stop by the ranch now and then, was actually her real father. 'I didn't believe him at first,' she explained, 'but he finally convinced me and said that he and Momma had always loved each other and would have gotten married except he couldn't make himself settle down. That's why she'd married Pa Mercer, my stepfather and had two sons by him.'

'And they were all killed?' I said.

Liberty nodded. I could barely see her face in the

near-darkness but by the sound of her voice I knew she still hadn't gotten over their loss.

Realizing she'd lost more than I had, I said: 'Did you cry a lot?'

'All the time,' she said. 'Till after the funeral. Then, it was like I was all cried-out and I stopped and didn't cry anymore. Though I still miss them and hurt when I think about them. Probably always will.'

'Wonder what's wrong with me?' I said, thinking aloud. 'I loved Pa and I already miss him but I can't cry and I don't feel sad, neither.'

'How do you feel?'

'I dunno.'

'Sure you do. Think.'

I thought. 'Kind of . . . numb and dead inside, I reckon.'

Liberty nodded as if understanding, 'You poor lamb,' put her arm around me and cuddled me to her. 'I wish there was something I could do to help.'

It's funny. The moment she said that, I got all my feelings back and started crying and thought I'd never stop.

CHAPTER NINE

The next morning was clear and sunny, but not too hot, and all around me in the cemetery I could hear people who'd come to mourn Pa saying what a great day this was for a funeral.

Uncle Del and Aunt Connie never showed. I was most likely the only person there that wasn't surprised. I wasn't too unhappy, either. Because though I knew eventually I'd still have to go live with them – *and their chickens* – it also meant that I might not go there immediately as Sheriff McAllister had been called to Deming to testify as a witness in a murder trial by some important lawyer. He had to leave on the noon train and as a result, couldn't take me to Uncle Del's as he'd intended. Neither could Deputy Meeks, since he was in Columbus picking up a prisoner.

'Does that mean I can go home for now?' I asked the sheriff as he and Liberty walked me back from the cemetery to his office.

'No,' he said. 'Deputy Mercer, here, has kindly agreed to take you.'

Surprised, I stopped and turned to Liberty. 'Thought you were going to Mexico after those men?'

'I am,' she replied. 'But the sheriff says I'll pass by your uncle's place on my way to the border, and I thought this would give us some extra time together. 'Sides, you'll need someone to help you load all your things onto a wagon. May as well be me as anyone. Of course,' she added, 'that's if you don't mind riding with me?'

I said I didn't – which was true. 'Cause though I would have sooner not gone at all, going with Liberty was, as Pa used to say, the best of two bads.

CHAPTER TEN

It was early afternoon when Liberty and I rode over the steep sandy rise that sloped down to our ranch. The sight of the low, adobe-brick house, plank-walled barn and the windmill pump between Ma's vegetable patch and the corral made me tear up. Or maybe it was the idea that Pa wasn't there waiting to tell me to fix supper, feed the chickens or sew a button on his shirt that upset me – I'm not sure. It might even have been the fact that this was most likely the last time I would see the ranch, or call it mine, since from what the sheriff told me I'd probably need to sell it and have a lawyer put the money in something called a trust, whatever that means.

Anyways, whatever the reason, I started crying and didn't stop completely until Liberty and I had loaded up the wagon with all the things I wanted to take to Uncle's Del's; then, as we hitched up the team and prepared to leave she said something that made me realize how much she not only cared about me but understood how I felt. She said: 'Before we leave, scout, why don't you spend a few minutes here alone? Maybe wander around a little or sit in the house and collect your thoughts?'

'Is that what you did?' I said, remembering what she'd told me about losing her family.

She nodded, face creased with pain and concern.

'Did it make you feel better?'

'Yes. It helped anyway. If nothing else, it gave me a chance to say a few private goodbyes.'

I sniffed back my tears and looked at the house. I didn't feel any urge to go in there. Then I felt my gaze pulled to the barn and, just like that, I knew exactly what I needed to do.

'I'll only be a few minutes,' I said as I started away.

'Take all the time you need,' she called after me.

In the barn I kneeled on the floor by the stalls where Pa had found Ma, after she'd collected all the fresh-laid eggs that Sunday morning, and closing my eyes, told her that if Pa wasn't already with her, he'd be there soon. Next I told her where I was going to be living from now on and for her not to worry about me as I would be fine – oh, and that I was going to keep on painting, like she wanted me to do, and that I hoped she'd be proud of me one day when my pictures were good enough for folks to buy. Finally I said I loved her and still missed her, more than anything, and hoped she'd be happy now that Pa was with her. I then said 'Amen,' and I went back outside and told

Liberty I was ready to start.

'Good,' she said. 'Then climb aboard and we'll make some dust.'

I obeyed her.

She finished tying our horses to the back of the wagon, then climbed up on the box seat beside me and snapped the reins. The team leaned into the traces . . . the wagon shuddered and rolled forward.

I took a final look back at the house and then faced front. I realized I'd stopped crying. Surprised, I turned to Liberty. 'Reckon you're right,' I said. 'Those private goodbyes you told me about, they did help.'

CHAPTER ELEVEN

We saw the smoke first – a black smudge curling upward on the flat, distant, heat-wavering horizon.

Liberty reined up the team, took off her old brown campaign hat and used it to shield her eyes from the sun. Squinting, she studied the smoke for a few moments then frowned and turned to me. 'Could that be your uncle's place? Or are there other ranches between here and his spread?'

Not wanting to believe what I was seeing, I numbly shook my head. 'None. It's his all right.'

That's all she needed to hear. 'Hang on, scout!' Lashing the horses with the reins, she forced them into a gallop, urging them on even faster with yells of encouragement. It wasn't much of a trail. The sun-baked ground was full of wheel-ruts and potholes, causing the speeding wagon to bounce around worse than a Mexican jumping bean. I clung on with both hands and braced my feet against the foot rest. Even so, I was sure I was going to be thrown off any second or, worse – that Pa's old wagon was going to break apart or a wheel was going to come loose and we'd overturn.

But I reckon Ma coaxed the good Lord into looking after us that day. Because though we had almost two miles to go, and we covered them faster than I would've thought possible, when Liberty eventually pulled the sweat-lathered horses to a slithering stop outside my uncle's house, I realized we'd made it in one piece.

That's when I got my first real look at the ranch. I couldn't believe my eyes. It looked like the Devil had paid a visit. The house, barn and rows of wood-and-wire chicken pens were in smoldering ruins. Thick smoke swirled around everything. It made my eyes sting and water and plugged up my nose. I looked about me. Dead chickens lay scattered everywhere. Most of them were shot to pieces. Worse, a dozen or more had been buried up to their necks and used for target practice. Every one of them had its head shot off. Horrified, I looked around for Uncle Del's dogs. Both lay dead on the front porch. I heard bleating. I looked toward the windmill. Two of the milk goats lay on their side, bleeding to death. Sickened, I turned away.

'Stay here,' Liberty said grimly. 'Don't get down till I tell you!'

Rifle in hand, she jumped off the wagon and warily looked about her.

Nothing moved.

It was so quiet I could hear the faint crackle of dying embers.

Terrified, I kept expecting men to jump out of nowhere and start shooting at us. At the same time I wondered where my aunt and uncle were and why there weren't any dead Mescaleros anywhere.

'Must've jumped them at night or when my uncle was just getting up.'

'What?'

I wasn't listening, either. 'Uncle Del's a good shot,' I said, thinking aloud. 'It's unlikely that he didn't kill any of them.' Looking around, I added: 'I don't see any arrows anywhere.'

'This wasn't Indians,' Liberty said disgustedly.

'How do you know? Pa says there's still a few rene-gades in the sierras 'cross the border.'

'I'm sure there is. But Indians – even renegades – would've taken the chickens with them. And the goats. So would've Mexicans. Only white men slaughter for the fun of it.'

She had not looked at me while talking. Now as she slowly moved to the south side of the still-smoldering house, she saw something that made her stiffen. I looked in the same direction and saw it hanging over the side of the water trough. It was charred black. At first I thought it was a stick or a rake handle. Then, as Liberty walked up to the trough and poked the 'stick' with her rifle, I saw a flash of pinkish-white and realized it was a human arm and hand.

I must have screamed because Liberty quickly spun around and ran back to me, saying: 'Stop it! Quiet down! Pull yourself together! Please,' she begged as I kept screaming, 'stop it! You hear me, scout? Get hold of yourself!'

I stopped screaming. But I couldn't talk, couldn't even breathe. I felt my chest heaving as I gasped and struggled for air.

Liberty dropped her rifle, grabbed me and pulled me off the wagon. I landed on her and we both went sprawling. I fought for air, couldn't get any and started to black out. That's when I felt a sudden stinging pain across my face. Then another. Lights exploded in my head. Shocked, I realized I could breathe again and sucked in great mouthfuls of air.

'Sorry,' Liberty said, helping me up. 'I didn't mean to hurt you. But you were turning blue and I was afraid you'd suffocate—'

'It-it's all right,' I said, realizing she'd slapped me. 'It didn't hurt much.'

She looked relieved. She turned for a moment and looked toward the water trough; then turning back to me, she put her arm around my shoulder and said quietly: 'I need you to be very brave. *Very* brave. You understand?'

I nodded and looked at the blackened arm hanging out of the trough. 'Is . . . is that. . . ?' I couldn't finish.

'Your uncle? I don't know. Did he have a reddish brown beard?'

I nodded. 'It's him, ain't it?' I said, forgetting my grammar.

' 'Fraid so.'

I'd never seen her look so grim. I tried not to cry but it was impossible to stop the tears.

Liberty tried her best to comfort me. But nothing she said helped.

Inside, I felt cold, empty and alone.

'W-What about Aunt Connie?' I asked. 'She dead too?'

'I don't know, scout.' Liberty let go of me and looked about her. 'Her body isn't in the trough but ... it's very possible ... even likely that whoever killed your uncle killed her too. We'll just have to keep looking.' She stared at all the dead chickens and the now-dead goats and though she didn't say anything, I knew that she was hoping Aunt Connie was dead, for her sake.

I said: 'It's them, ain't it? Those three men you're after?'

'That'd be my guess, yes. 'Least, two of them anyway.'

'Why only two of them?'

She sighed and shook her head, as if in disbelief.

'What is it?' I said. Then: 'Tell me, please.'

'The other man, Latigo Rawlins, I don't think he'd do something like this.'

'Why not?'

'Because ... I know him.'

'You know a murderer – an escaped convict?'

She nodded and looked sort of ashamed. 'It was a long time ago . . . I was only sixteen and still at St Mark's . . . Latigo used to come and see me . . . I liked him, even though he was much older than me . . . and I would sneak out at night to be with him. . . .'

'Was he a murderer then?'

She didn't answer me. 'Lat' knew my father . . . they were friends, old friends, though Daddy disapproved of him.' She paused, frowning as if she too disapproved, then said: 'At the time Lat' was a bounty hunter and a hired gun working for Mr Stadtlander—'

'Yet you still liked him?'

'I did. I know it's hard to believe – I find it hard to believe myself now, but—' She stopped in mid-sentence and cocked her head toward the house, as if listening for something. 'You hear that?' she asked.

I nodded. 'Sounded like someone calling out.'

Liberty levered a round into the magazine of her Winchester, said, 'Stay behind me, y'hear?' and led the way alongside of the still-smoking remains of the house.

CHAPTER TWELVE

I followed Liberty around behind the smoldering ruins and saw a sight that I will never forget, no matter how old or touched in the head I get.

Staked out on a low mound was a man. He was naked, head-to-toe, which is something I'd never seen before. He was kind of small and lean, with curly sandy-colored hair and cruel yellow eyes like a wolf. At first I thought he was wearing some sort of dark reddish undershirt. But as I got closer and noticed he was squirming around, head flopping from side to side, I realized it wasn't a shirt or even paint – it was ants!

I felt sick and turning away, almost threw up.

Liberty spun around, looking as horrified as I felt, and stood in front of me so that I couldn't see the man. 'Go get one of the blankets from the wagon,' she exclaimed. 'And bring my canteen. Hurry! Run! Run!'

I ran.

I was only gone a few minutes. But when I returned with the blanket and canteen she had already cut the man loose and was once more shielding him with her body. Grabbing the blanket from me, 'Turn around and don't look till I tell you,' she handed it to the man.

I obeyed. I heard him grunting with pain as they both quickly brushed the ants from him, his voice so hoarse he could barely speak.

'All right,' Liberty told me presently. 'You can look.'

I did. The man now had the blanket wrapped around him. Liberty took the canteen from me, unscrewed the top and tilted it up to his mouth. He drank greedily, water spilling down his stubbly chin. His lips were cracked and from what I'd seen earlier he was bleeding all over from thousands of ant bites. He was also badly sunburned, the skin blistered in places.

'That's enough for now,' Liberty said, lowering the canteen. 'Can have some more in a few minutes.'

'P-Pour some over my head,' he begged hoarsely.

Liberty did as he asked. He winced as the water washed over the bites. 'Sonofabitch!' he hissed. 'Feels like I on fire.'

'Watch your mouth in front of the child,' Liberty chided. Then to me: 'Hope, go wait for us in the wagon, please.'

'First I want to ask him somethin',' I said.

'Can't it wait?'

I ignored her question and said angrily to the man: 'Mister, did you kill my uncle and aunt?'

He weakly shook his head. I didn't believe him. But I said anyway: 'You see who did?'

'Men I was runnin' with.'

'You mean Dano and Canfield?' Liberty said.

'Yeah. I tried to stop 'em, just like I tried to stop 'em from raping the woman, but the bastards jumped me an'—' He collapsed, so suddenly that Liberty couldn't catch him and he fell to the ground.

'Go bring the wagon and horses around,' Liberty told me. 'Go on,' she added when I didn't move. 'This man's Latigo Rawlins. I need to keep him alive.'

When I got back with the wagon, Latigo was wearing Levi's and socks and sitting on the ground gingerly pulling on his boots. Liberty explained that they'd found his things in the brush where the outlaws had thrown them. I asked where his shirt was and she said that it had been torn off and was in pieces. As she talked, she went to her horse that was still tied behind the wagon next to mine and took a spare shirt from her saddle-bags. 'You can wear this,' she told Latigo, 'till you get another one.'

He grunted his thanks and after drinking some more water, managed to get up on his own. He winced every time he moved. Looking at all the bites covering his sunburned flesh made me wince, too. I mean I know he was a gunman, a killer who'd escaped from prison, but I would've had to have been made of stone not to feel sorry for him.

' 'Fore you put that shirt on, mister,' I said, 'you ought to rub grease on all those bites. It'll help take the sting away.'

He looked at me with his odd-colored yellow eyes like he was seeing me, proper, for the first time. 'You got some grease, missy?'

'Pa does,' I said, forgetting that he was dead. 'All right if I fetch it?' I asked Liberty. When she nodded, I climbed onto the wagon, opened the box seat and took out the can of axle grease that Pa always kept there.

Returning beside Latigo I unscrewed the lid and let him scoop out some grease. The heat had melted it, making it easy to use. Most of the bites were on his chest, neck and face. When he was all done rubbing grease on them, he wiped his hands clean on his torn shirt and gave me a long, curious look.

'Much 'bliged to you, missy. That's the first kind thing anybody's done for me in almost ten years.'

'That how long you been in prison?' I said.

He nodded. 'Longer than you been born, most likely.'

'Almost,' I said. 'I'll be eleven end of next month.'

'Eleven,' he repeated, as if he couldn't believe anyone was that young. 'Man alive, sure wish to Christ I was eleven again.'

'Well you're not,' Liberty said crossly. 'So quit dreaming about a fresh start and put that shirt on. There's a jail waiting for you in Columbus and I'm anxious to get you in it, so I can get started after your gutless murdering pals.'

'You want Dano an' Canfield,' Latigo said, easing himself into the shirt, 'jail's the last place I should be.'

Liberty snorted. 'If you're suggesting I make a deal with you, you must think I'm dumber than when you first met me.'

I could tell she was really angry about something and wondered what it was.

'You weren't dumb, Emily,' Latigo said, nicer than I expected from a killer. 'Young maybe, even naïve, but never dumb.'

'Dumb enough to trust you,' she said. 'But never again.' Stepping to her horse, she took a pair of wrist-irons from her saddle-bags and returned to Latigo. 'Now give me your hands.'

'Suit yourself.' He stuck out his wrists and she fastened the irons about them. 'But you're makin' a mistake. I could lead you right to them. What's more, way I feel about those no-good bastards, I'd gladly help you round 'em up.'

'Thanks, but no thanks.'

'They ain't alone, you know. Countin' the no-goods who were waitin' here for them, an' the rest of their old gang holed up across the border, you could be facin' more fifteen twenty men.'

'I said, no thanks.'

Not wanting her to get killed by more outlaws than she could handle, I said: 'Maybe you ought to listen to him. I mean if someone staked me out over a bunch of ants, I'd want to get back at them too.'

'Look,' Liberty said, trying to be patient, 'I know you mean well, scout, but you don't know this man – what he's capable of. He gets his hands on a gun he's just as likely to shoot us as anyone else.'

'You know that ain't true,' Latigo said. 'I walked out on you once 'cause I couldn't bear to hurt you – time in prison ain't changed nothin' between us.'

'Well, you're right about one thing,' Liberty said. 'There definitely is nothing between us – not now or ever again!'

Latigo sighed and his whole body sagged, like he'd run out of life.

'So what happens next?' he asked.

'I already told you: I'm taking you to Columbus and—'

I had to know something, badly enough to interrupt her. 'What about me?' I asked. 'You leaving me in Columbus too?'

'Yes. With the sheriff. I'll have him find someone responsible to take you back to Santa Rosa. Or, if luck's with us,' she added, 'and Deputy Meeks hasn't picked up his prisoner yet, I'll ask him to escort you.'

'And what happens to me then,' I demanded, 'when I'm in Santa Rosa? I mean I've got no one to go to. Who's going to look after me?'

'I really don't know,' Liberty said, frustrated. 'Right now, scout, I got more things than I can handle as is.'

'You wouldn't,' Latigo put in, 'not if you'd let me an' Gabe help you.'

'Gabe?' she said, frowning. 'What the hell's Gabriel Moonlight got to do with it?'

'He's holed up in Chihuahua an' I know how to find him. If he threw in with us, like I know he would, his gun would help even out the odds a little. Might even save your life.'

Liberty hated the idea – yet at the same time I could tell she was giving it a lot of thought. Then she shook her head.

'No, that's a crazy idea. I don't even know Gabe that well. Why would he risk his neck for me?'

'You know the answer to that, same as I do.'

'My father?'

'He's known Gabe almost as long as I have – what's more, they ain't had the fallin' outs we've had on occasion. But you already know that, Emily, 'cause it was Gabe who helped you'n Drifter get your horses back from the Comancheros.'

Liberty didn't say anything. She didn't have to. Everything was right there to see, painted on her face.

It was then Latigo drove the last nail home. 'Somethin' else you should know,' he said. 'The good-lookin' gal that was here – your aunt, I reckon,' he said to me, '—after they got done raping her, they took her along with 'em. For sport, Dano said. But that ain't the only reason. When they're done with her, they plan to sell what's left of her to one of the

71

cantinas, so she can earn her keep.'

I gritted my teeth and nervously played with my braids, trying not to picture what was going to happen to Aunt Connie.

Liberty looked contemptuously at Latigo. 'You bastard,' she said. 'You won't stop at anything to get your way, will you?'

'Not when it comes to you, no,' he said. 'Everythin' else rolls off my back like water off a goose.'

CHAPTER THIRTEEN

We buried Uncle Del on a low, scrub-covered rise behind the barn. It was his favorite place to sit and watch the sun go down. I said some words over him, mostly just thanking him for treating me kindly, and then helped Liberty and Latigo shovel dirt back on top of the body. I also made a cross from two sticks I found and wedged it in between the rocks we used to protect the grave from animals. I knew in time the dust storms would blow it away but at least it was there for now and I knew that would make Pa and Ma happy.

We started out for Columbus. It's a far piece and I knew we'd have to camp overnight and then continue on to the *pueblo* the next morning. I'd never been there but had heard folks talk about it, most dismissing it as nothing more than a 'grubby little eyesore' located thirty miles south of Deming. The men who left Latigo to die had taken his horse, so I had to ride double behind Liberty while he rode my chestnut. He was still wearing wrist-irons that Liberty had tied to the saddle horn, and she still refused to let him help her track down the escaped convicts; but as the day wore on and we stopped now and then to give the horses a blow and to swallow a little water and chew on jerky, I sensed she was slowly warming to the idea of letting him lead her to her Pa's old friend – Gabriel Moonlight.

We rode until sundown. Then as dusk settled in and overhead swarms of bats began darting around after insects, we made camp inside a circle of ancient rocks that over time the wind had worn into strange twisted shapes. I started a fire and Liberty unsaddled the horses while Latigo, still handcuffed, spread our blankets on the still-warm ground.

He kept looking at Liberty and I figured he was going to ask her to remove his irons, but he didn't. Nor did Liberty offer. She got busy making a pot of coffee, not once looking at him, and then we all sat around the fire eating jerky and hardtack without saying a word. It was kind of eerie and made me uncomfortable. I felt like both of them wished I wasn't there so they could have it out and settle whatever it was that was chewing on them. I tried to start a conversation with Liberty, but I could tell she wasn't interested in talking; so I sat there in glum silence, dunking my biscuit in my coffee. I don't usually like coffee because it's too bitter, but Liberty added cinnamon to hers and I ended up drinking two cups.

It was while I was pouring the second cup that Liberty, who'd barely spoken to Latigo during the ride, must have decided to trust him. I say that because she got up, unlocked his wrist-irons and put them in her saddle-bags.

For a moment he was as surprised as I was. Then, rubbing his chafed wrists, he said quietly: 'I'll need a gun.'

It sounded like a harmless remark to me, but for some reason Liberty took exception to it. 'When I think you need a gun,' she snapped, 'I'll give you one.'

Latigo shrugged, as if that was OK with him, and that seemed to make her even angrier. Shooting him a cold, hard look, she said through her teeth: 'There's something you ought to know. If I live to be a hundred, I'll never forgive you for killing Liberty.'

'Didn't expect you to.'

'What's more,' she seethed, 'no matter how this turns out, if we're still alive after it's over, I'm taking you back to Huntsville. That clear?'

'Perfectly. Anythin' else?'

'No.'

'OK then,' Latigo said, smiling like Pa used to when he was holding two pair. 'Now that my future's settled, how 'bout we forget our differences an' work together from now on?'

'I'll think on it,' Liberty said. She threw her coffee dregs onto the embers, making them sizzle. 'Meanwhile, Mr Rawlins, you stay on your side of the fire and tomorrow keep riding ahead of me. That way I won't have any reason to shoot you.'

CHAPTER FOURTEEN

It was early morning when we rode into Columbus. The sun was already hot on our necks and the wind, which everybody grumbles about, was churning up the dust and blowing tumbleweeds everywhere. Two of them bounced along the dirt street that led us between the scattered shacks, seedy cantinas and stores facing the railroad tracks. From what I've been told, Mexico was only a short ride beyond those tracks – and holed up somewhere in Mexico were the two men who'd murdered Uncle Del and stolen Aunt Connie.

Just thinking about them and what they'd done made me boiling mad.

We rode on through town. I hadn't expected much but this place was even worse than I expected. As I clung on behind Liberty, squinting against the swirling dust, I tried to find something worthwhile to paint. When nothing interested me, I looked at the people on the street. There were only a few and most of them were Mexicans. I don't know if it was because I was sad and depressed myself but the men and women we passed looked unhappy too. I noticed it on their brown, weathered faces and in their dark, sad eyes, as well as in the defeated way they went about their daily chores.

Ahead, where the street ended and, according to Liberty, hooked up with the trail to Deming, stood the jail – a small, one-story adobe building with a single iron door and no windows. An old, bare-footed Mexican, his face hidden under a floppy-brimmed sombrero, was painting the walls a muddy yellow color.

Liberty and Latigo reined up outside the door and dismounted. I jumped down behind them and watched as Liberty tried the door. It was locked. She turned to the old Mexican, who hadn't bothered to look at us, and asked him where the sheriff was.

He stopped painting, tipped back his sombrero and looked at us, his wrinkly, leathery face as old as the desert. '*Yo no hablo Ingles*,' he said.

'I'll ask him,' I said, anxious to help. Then to the old man: '*Señor, donde esta el sheriff?*'

'*En algun lugar de las Tres Hermanas, Pequena.*'

'*Que esta haciendo hasta en las montanas?*'

'*Buscando a un ladron.*'

'*Cuando el volvera?*'

'*No se, Pequena. Dos quiza tres dias.*' He tilted his

sombrero forward and went on painting.

I turned to Liberty. 'Did you understand him?'

'Some of it – sheriff's up in the mountains or something. But you better tell me everything. My Spanish is pretty rusty.'

'Says the sheriff is looking for a robber or a thief, I'm not quite sure which, in the mountains just north of here called the Three Sisters. Won't be back for two maybe three days.'

Liberty nodded. 'OK, so now all we have to do is find out if Deputy Meeks was here and picked up his prisoner.'

'What're you going to do if he has? – with me, I mean?'

'I don't know,' she said, frustrated. Then to Latigo: 'Any ideas?'

'Bring her along,' he said. 'There's a woman I know in Palomas. For a few pesos she'll look after the kid.'

Liberty looked at him like the sun had melted his brains. '*Palomas*?' she said. 'Good Christ, Latigo! Palomas is nothing but a hellhole full of outlaws, drunks and whores. I wouldn't leave a dead coyote to rot there.'

Latigo shrugged and gently rubbed his ant-bitten neck. 'Just a suggestion, Emily. No need to throw a loop. 'Sides, Maria's no whore. She cooks at one of the cantinas there. Has young'uns of her own to raise. Reckon she'd be happy to have someone like Hope to help her with the chores, is all I was thinkin'.'

'I don't mind,' I said. 'I'll do anything to help you catch the killers.'

'Thanks. I appreciate that,' Liberty said, ruffling my hair. 'But it wouldn't work. I'd be worrying about you all the time, and that's dangerous when you're going after men like Canfield and Dano. No,' she added, sighing, 'there's got to be a better solution than that.' Turning to the old Mexican, she asked him in Spanish if a gringo deputy sheriff from Santa Rosa had been there yesterday to pick up a prisoner.

He thought a moment then humbly removed his hat and hung his white-haired head as if ashamed. 'I beg your forgiveness, *señorita*, but I do not know if this is true. There is a man, however, who might know of such a thing.'

'What's his name, *señor*, and where can I find him?'

Turned out the man's name was Doke Ingram and he tended bar at the Las Flores, one of the ratty cantinas we'd passed on our way in. He was a big, surly man with a nose like a badger and a pock-marked face. He wasn't happy to see us, I could tell that by his scowl as he saw us walk in, and he got even surlier when Liberty showed him her deputy marshal's star and questioned him about Deputy Meeks.

'Yeah, he was here yesterday,' he growled, 'no-good sonofabitch.'

'Sounds like you had a run-in with him.'

'Bastard bent his six-killer over my goddamn

head.' He leaned forward over the bar and parted his black hair to show a newly-stitched gash on his scalp. 'Doc Rivera, he says any deeper an' it would've cracked my skull wide open – maybe done me in.'

Latigo said: 'No offense, *amigo*, but I know Meeks. Moves slower'n molasses an' got a temper to match. You must've truly rubbed him raw for him to pound on you like that.'

'I didn't rub him any way, mister. Just tried to reason with him. Prisoner he come for was my nephew, Seth. He ain't no outlaw, just a thimble-brained kid.'

'Who was caught driving cattle – *another man's cattle* – across the border,' Liberty reminded.

'Seth didn't know they belonged to nobody. Figured they was strays. Said it was too dark to see if they were burned by an iron.'

Latigo chuckled. 'Reckon next time he'll know to do his rustlin' durin' daylight hours.'

Laughter came from the men along the bar who'd been listening.

The bartender gave him a murderous look, 'Mister, you got a smart mouth needs closin',' and I saw him reach below the bar.

'Latigo!' I shouted.

But he'd already seen the bartender going for his hidden gun and his left hand, moving almost too fast to see, grabbed a half-empty bottle of tequila from the bar and broke it across the big man's face. Blood and broken teeth spattered everywhere. The bartender

81

collapsed behind the bar.

Liberty instantly levered a shell into her rifle and aimed it at the men facing her. 'Easy, *hombres* . . . easy. . . .'

The men froze, but continued to glare at her.

Holding the rifle with one hand, she drew her Colt .45 and tossed it to Latigo. Catching it, he covered the rest of the customers, most of whom had risen from their tables and were closing in menacingly on Liberty.

'That's close enough,' he said. Then to Liberty: 'Your call, Marshal.'

'We're done here,' she said. Gesturing for the men along the bar to step back, she motioned for me to leave. I obeyed. But when I reached the door, I stopped and held it open for her and Latigo. Both of them backed up toward me, guns covering everyone in the cantina. Latigo came out first and untied the horses. Back turned to me, Liberty paused in the doorway and warned everyone that she'd shoot anybody who followed us.

No one moved or said anything. But I could feel their rage.

Liberty backed out, door swinging shut behind her, and the two of us hurried to the horses. Mounting first, she pulled me up behind her and dug in her spurs. Latigo did the same and we galloped off down the street.

I glanced back to see if anyone was following us. They weren't.

Shortly, we reached the edge of town. Crossing the railroad tracks, we followed the trail leading to the border. But we had only ridden a short distance when Liberty reined up and held out her hand to Latigo. 'I'll take my gun back now.'

His face darkened and for a moment I thought he wasn't going to obey her. Then he pulled the Colt out of his jeans and handed it to her. Liberty holstered it and dragged her Winchester from its scabbard. 'Here,' she said, giving it to him. 'Keep this till we get you a pistol.'

'*Gracias.*' Latigo tucked the rifle under the saddle. 'Gabe's probably got an extra Colt or two stashed away I can use.'

We rode on. Knowing we were no longer welcome in Columbus, I figured I'd dodged a bullet. Maybe if my luck held, this Gabriel Moonlight fella wouldn't know what to do with me either.

Liberty, as if reading my mind, said: 'Looks like you'll be coming with us, scout – 'least for now.'

'I don't mind,' I said, trying not to sound too pleased. 'I promise not to get in your way.'

'I'm not worried about my way,' she said. 'It's harm's way that concerns me.'

I had no answer for that. So I just clung to her, head resting on her back, and tried to imagine what being in Mexico was going to be like.

MEXICO

CHAPTER FIFTEEN

Nuevo Cadiz was a hot dusty village nestled in the foothills that, according to Latigo, was about an hour's ride north of Gabriel Moonlight's cabin.

The trail to get there wasn't too steep, which was lucky because all our horses were getting weary, Liberty's bay especially.

As we entered the little *pueblo*, following one of the narrow dirt streets that led to the plaza, the villagers we rode past gave us suspicious, menacing looks. When I asked Latigo why they were so unfriendly, he explained that Gabe had been holed up in a nearby valley since his early outlaw days. During those years he had protected them from marauding *bandidos*, paid for the church and the school to be repaired after an earthquake and once, during a long drought, brought a professional well-digger all the way from Juarez to dig for new wells. For this he'd earned the respect and affection of the villagers who now considered him to be their *patrón* and didn't want any *gringo* lawmen coming here to take him away.

'Why would they think Liberty's a lawman?' I asked. 'She took off her star like you told her to, and there's no government brand on her horse.'

'But there *is* the faded outline of a star on her shirt, an' another on her jacket where she usually wears it,' he replied, 'an' for sharp eyes that's a dead giveaway.'

The three of us were dismounting outside a cantina as he spoke, and I looked at Liberty and realized he was right about the outline. Ashamed of myself for not noticing it before, it reminded me of how much I still had to learn about being observant, as Ma called it, if I wanted to be a true artist like Mr Remington was.

A sign said the cantina served food. Since we were all hungry we sat outside at one of the wobbly-legged tables that was shaded by the roof overhang and wolfed down plates of black beans and rice and sopped up the gravy with fresh-made tortillas. An old woman in a yellow and red flowered dress stood beside a brick oven, making the tortillas. I watched her as I ate, thinking how much I'd love to paint her – especially her face, which was as wrinkled as a dead leaf in winter.

Behind the woman, across the sun-scorched street facing a beautiful old stone fountain honoring the Madonna, stood another cantina. It didn't have any tables out front but it did have a hitch-rail, and tied to it were two horses with western saddles. One was a regular cowpony but the other was an old but mag-nificent-looking black stallion that whenever one of the passing villagers got too close, tried to bite them. No one got bitten, but it was funny to see them jump back as the stallion took a swipe at them.

'What's so amusing?' Liberty asked as I giggled.

'That black horse.' I pointed. 'It keeps trying to bite—'

'Oh-my-God,' she said softly as she saw the two horses.

'What, what?' Latigo asked. He followed her gaze and saw the horses himself. 'Jesus-on-a-cross,' he breathed. 'I don't believe it.'

'Where you goin'?' I demanded as they both jumped up.

'Wait here,' Liberty said. 'Be right back.' She and Latigo hurried across the street and, keeping clear of the black stallion, entered the cantina.

I didn't move right away. But then I noticed some of the villagers had seen them enter the cantina and were now talking angrily among themselves, pointing at me and then at the cantina as if they were upset.

That's was enough for me. Wiping my plate clean with the last tortilla, I stuffed it in my mouth and ran across the street to the cantina. It had bat-wing doors and kneeling down I looked under them and saw Liberty, with Latigo right behind her, march up to a table in back and angrily wag her finger at one of the two men sitting, drinking, there.

'What the hell're you doing here?' I heard her say.

The man, who was old enough to be her father and kind of resembled her, was so shocked he didn't know what to say. By his bleary eyes, week-old stubble and sloppy grin I guessed he'd helped empty the two tequila bottles sitting in front of them – and probably others besides – and rather than meet Liberty's accusing glare he looked down at the shot glass he was twisting around between his fingers.

'Goo' question, Miss Emily,' said the tall, dark-haired man beside him. 'Wha' *are* you doin' here, Drifter?'

'Why I'm jus' visitin' an ol' pal,' the man called Drifter said.

'And the cutting horses you're supposed to be raising,' Liberty said. 'Who are they visiting?'

Ignoring her sarcasm, Drifter said: 'Fella gets bored by his lonesome. Needs a break from time to time.'

'I see,' Liberty said icily. 'So you decided to relieve your boredom by riding down here to get drunk and maybe chase the rabbit a little?'

'Reckon that's one way of lookin' at it.' Drifter grinned sheepishly. 'Wha' are *you* doin' here, by the way?'

'What I'm doing, *father*, is wondering why the hell

you aren't at home, taking care of our stock, like you're damn' well supposed to be doing!'

'I tol' you, I got bored,' Drifter said. 'Wouldn't begrudge your ol' man a little tequila, would you?'

Latigo chuckled – then abruptly fell silent as Liberty glared at him.

'Dammit, Daddy, who's looking after the ranch?'

'The ranch?' Drifter said. 'Who's lookin' after the. . . ?' He paused, blinking owlishly, then said: 'That's a goo' ques'ion, too.'

'How about answering it?'

'Yessss, that's what I should do all right. Answer your ques'ion.' He sighed, his expelled breath puckering his lips. 'Wel-l-l,' he said finally, 'to answer your ques'ion: I'm not at the ranch 'cause I hired these two ol' boys I know – wranglers I used to break broomtails with. Said they'd be only too happy to handle things for grub and a place to sleep. Sooo, here I am.' He smiled brightly, seemingly pleased by his answer, and then said: 'Can't 'spect me to be in two places at once, now can you, daughter mine?'

For a moment I thought Liberty might grab one of the empty bottles and hit him with it. Instead, she disgustedly threw up her hands, 'Ohh-hh,' and turned to Latigo. 'You deal with him. I can't.' She spun around and marched to the bar, telling the short balding bartender: 'Tequila, *por favor.*'

That's when I heard footsteps behind me. Turning, I saw about a dozen villagers, *campesinos* in grubby white cotton field clothes, straw sombreros

88

pulled low over their grim faces, coming toward me – all of them armed with either old Mexican army rifles, machetes or pitchforks.

Crawling under the bat-wing doors, I jumped up and ran to Liberty. 'Outside,' I said, thumbing over my shoulders. 'W-We got company.'

CHAPTER SIXTEEN

It took a while to convince the villagers that their beloved *patrón* was not in danger of being arrested, hanged or taken back to the United States; but once they understood that, and realized who Liberty and Latigo were (no one seemed to notice me), they humbly apologized and returned to their fields.

'Maybe you should run for president down here,' Latigo joked to Gabe. 'I always wanted to live in a palace in Mexico City.'

'Goo' idea,' Gabe replied. 'Then next time there's a revolution an' the farmers decide to overthrow the government, we can all hang together.'

'A soberin' thought,' Drifter said. 'Let's vote on it.'

'You're drunk, Daddy,' Liberty chided.

'I surely hope so,' he said. 'Be a goddamn shame to waste all this tequila on someone sober.' Rising, he kissed her on the cheek and walked unsteadily to the door.

'Hey,' Gabe yelled, 'where you goin', *amigo?*'

'Strai'den out my brains,' Drifter said. He waved goodbye and staggered out. Almost immediately there was a loud splash.

We all looked at each other and then hurried to the window.

Outside, not far from the cantina, Drifter lay submerged in the Madonna fountain, only his head showing above the water.

'That sneaky sumbitch,' Gabe said, scowling. 'He's tryin' to steal my woman!' He staggered out before anyone could stop him.

We watched through the window as Gabe stumbled to the fountain, kissed the Madonna statue on the forehead like she was his girlfriend and collapsed into the water beside Drifter.

'Shouldn't we go out there?' I said, worried. 'Once when Pa was drunk, he fell in the water trough and almost drowned.'

'All the more reason we should stay in here,' Liberty said darkly. I couldn't tell if she was joking or not, but after a few moments she fondly ruffled my hair and went outside.

'Reckon I'll go join 'em,' Latigo said. 'Maybe a cold bath'll stop these bites from itchin'.' He winked at me and walked out.

I stood there looking out the window, watching as Latigo joined Gabe and Drifter floating in the fountain. He must have said something that riled them, because the three of them suddenly began splashing each other like ducks in a pond. Liberty jumped back but it was too late: she was already soaked. Angry, she started hollering at them. But they only laughed and splashed her some more. That really set her off. Jumping into the fountain, she splashed the men back. Her father teamed up with her and pretty soon it turned into a real water fight.

Watching them have so much fun made me jealous. I'd never seen four grown-ups enjoy themselves like that before and I wished I was out there with them. But then I got a better idea. Taking out this little stubby pencil I always keep in my shirt pocket I got a piece of paper from the bartender and returning to the window, quickly sketched everyone laughing and splashing each other in the fountain.

I knew how much shooting and killing there was going to be when Liberty tried to capture the men who'd killed my uncle and kidnapped Aunt Connie – and figured I better draw a picture of them all together, having fun, in case something bad was to happen to any of them.

Everyone soon dried off in the hot sun. Then we all crossed over and sat around one of the outside tables at the other cantina. Here Liberty told Gabe and her father – who were now sober – why she and Latigo were there. She then explained why I was with them and asked Gabe if he knew of anyone who'd be willing to look after me for a few days. He thought a moment then offered to talk to the local padre, Father Ignacio, adding that he may know of a family willing to take care of me. And if the priest didn't, then maybe he could be persuaded to let me stay with him at the church.

I didn't want to stay with the priest, or with anyone else for that matter. But naturally, no one asked my opinion and I knew better than to offer it. Truth is I was surprised that I was even allowed to stay and listen while they talked – being a young'un – but unlike Pa, no one seemed to object to me being there and of course I kept quieter than quail hiding in a bush.

As I listened I kept watching how everyone's expression changed during the conversation, so I'd know in future how to draw someone who was angry or happy or sad or even frustrated. It was a real lesson for me. I reckon I learned more about drawing people's faces in those two or three hours than if I'd gone to art school, like Ma wanted, for a year.

It was late afternoon by the time everyone said their piece. By then Gabe and Drifter had insisted on accompanying Liberty and Latigo to Palomas to help capture or kill Canfield and Dano and the gunmen who'd shot my uncle . . . and after that, hopefully, rescue my aunt.

'That's if she's still alive,' said Latigo.

Immediately Liberty shot him a nasty look before saying to me: 'Don't worry, scout – she will be.'

I nodded, like I believed her, but truthfully I didn't. It seemed like everyone I loved sooner or later died or got taken away from me and, deep down, I didn't think it would be any different with Aunt Connie.

'So how many guns we up against?' Gabe said. 'Six – eight – what?'

'More like fifteen,' Liberty said.

'Sounds like fair odds,' Gabe said.

He was joking but no one laughed.

'Could even be more than that,' Latigo said. 'Canfield use to ride with Quantril's Raiders durin' the war, an' he's got mighty grand plans.'

'Like what?'

'Recruitin' a bunch of the local gunmen an' then raiding an' looting the towns along the border, same way Quantril did in Kansas.'

'Jesus,' Drifter said. 'Nice company you keep, Lefty.'

Latigo shrugged. 'Ain't a lot of choir boys at Huntsville, *amigo*. On top of that,' he added, 'we might have to deal with a Gardner gun.'

'A what?' Gabe asked.

'Gardner gun. It's a machine gun, made by some officer during the Civil War.'

Drifter, Liberty and Gabe exchanged uneasy looks.

'Where the hell would they get a Gardner gun?' Drifter said.

'Supposedly, from two deserters who stole it from the post they were at. From what Dano said, the army was running tests on it to see if they wanted to buy it.'

Liberty, who'd noticed her father growing more

and more concerned, said: 'You think I should call this off, don't you?'

'Might be the smart thing to do,' he admitted.

She chewed on that for moment before saying: 'You said the same thing when I was sixteen and determined to get *El Diablo* and the mares back from the Comancheros.'

'Well,' Drifter said drily, ' 'least I ain't gotten dumber in my old age.'

'And I haven't gotten any less stubborn.'

Drifter shrugged. 'You asked my opinion, Emily – I gave it. Now it's up to you to do what you want.'

Liberty looked shrewdly at her father. Though she didn't show it, I sensed she was boiling inside. I was right. After glaring at him for a few moments, she said through clenched teeth:

'Why don't you say what's *really* on your mind?'

I could tell he didn't want to argue with her, but nor did he like to be prodded.

'All right,' he said quietly. 'Your stubbornness got a man killed an' for what? A bunch of mares that you ended up givin' away anyway.'

'I didn't give them away, Father – I traded them for our lives – yours, mine and Gabe's, here.'

'I know that. I also know how much the mares meant to you – an' Gabe an' me will always be grateful for the sacrifice—'

'But?'

'If you hadn't been so all-fired determined to go after the damn' mares in the first place, neither Gabe nor me – nor Lonnie Forbes – would have come to Mexico.'

'Except when you want to get drunk and chase the rabbit a little.'

Stung, Drifter went white but somehow controlled his temper.

'I'm sorry,' Liberty said, instantly regretting her words. 'That was disrespectful and for that I apologize.' Before he could say anything, she turned to Latigo and Gabe, adding: 'If you want to change your minds and pull out, I'll understand.'

Latigo said grimly: 'You forgettin' those two bastards left me to die over an ants' nest?'

'How about you?' Liberty asked Gabe.

He smiled – a smile that if I'd been older would've made my heart start pumping – and said: 'Like I told you that time in Blanco Canyon, when the *bandidos* had us trapped an' you let loose your mares: I'm still lookin' for the bullet with my name on it.'

'You never told me that,' Liberty said.

'I didn't?'

'No. That's something I would have remembered.'

'Well, I was thinkin' it, anyway.'

'Heroes,' Drifter grumbled. 'I'm surrounded by a bunch of two-bit Buntline heroes!'

Gabe chuckled, 'I'll drink to that,' and refilled their mugs from an earthen pitcher of beer.

'To heroes,' he toasted.

'Dead heroes,' Drifter said as everyone raised their mugs.

'Daddy – for God's sake!' exclaimed Liberty.

'It's a joke,' her father protested. He looked at me. 'You knew it was a joke, didn't you, Hope?'

'Yes, sir,' I said. But of course I was lying.

CHAPTER SEVENTEEN

The small, white adobe church faced the plaza. It was a fine church, not as grand or big as the churches in Santa Rosa, but bigger than any of the stores or houses surrounding it and I surely wouldn't have minded saying my prayers in it.

Now, as the four of us rode up to the entrance and dismounted, Father Ignacio was standing in the shade cast by the bell-tower, talking to a young, sad-faced woman holding a baby. On seeing Gabe, he excused himself and came hurrying up to us.

I liked him right off. He wasn't much taller than me, looked skinny in his black, ankle-length robe and wore hand-woven *huaraches* that were so old they flopped as he walked. But he had lots of silvery curls, warm friendly eyes that were as brown as his skin and a smile that made you want to trust him.

Gabe introduced him to us and then the two of

them went into the church to talk. While Drifter and Latigo leaned against the horses and rolled a smoke, Liberty pulled me aside and hunkered down in front of me so that our eyes were level. She had that look that grown-ups get when they're trying to think of how to tell you something they know you won't like.

Feeling sorry for her, I said: 'It's all right. I know you can't take me with you.'

'I truly can't,' she said. 'I want to – I mean I don't want to leave you, here or anywhere else, but. . . .'

'It's all right,' I repeated numbly. 'I understand.'

'Afterwards,' she said as if she hadn't heard me, 'when this is all over and you're back with your aunt in Santa Rosa, I'll come and visit you. That's a promise.'

'I'd like that,' I said.

'I'd like it too, scout. Truly I would.' She kissed me on the forehead, her lips cool and damp despite the heat, then straightened up, took my hand and led me back to Latigo and her father.

'I was just tellin' Latigo,' Drifter said to Liberty. 'When we're done here an' get back home, maybe Hope, here, would like to come an' stay with us for a spell.'

'I'm sure she would,' Liberty began – then stopped as Gabe came out of the church. He looked troubled. We waited for him to say something. When he didn't, Liberty said impatiently: 'Well? What did Father Ignacio say?'

'He's more'n willin' to look after her,' Gabe said.

99

'But—?'

'He can't do it right away.'

'Why not?' Drifter asked.

' 'Cause he's ridin' up into the hills tomorrow to spend time with the local Indians. He only converted 'em recently an' has to go up there every so often to remind 'em why they should be Christians.'

'Damn,' Liberty said, making a face.

'Sorry,' said Gabe, adding: 'He offered to take Hope with him but warned me that there's *bandidos* in the hills, so I told him no thanks. 'Course it's up to you, Emily, but—'

'No, no, you did the right thing. Thanks.' Liberty sighed, frustrated, and toed the dirt with her boot.

Drifter, Latigo and Gabe swapped 'What now?' looks.

Latigo looked at me, then at Liberty. 'Why don't you look after her?'

'Mean take her with us? You can't be serious.'

'Let me finish. The four of us ride to the outskirts of Palomas. Then you an' she can hole up somewhere while me, Gabe and Drifter ride on in an' take care of Canfield, Dano an' the others.'

'That's not a bad idea,' Drifter said.

'It's a goddamn good one, y'ask me,' Gabe said.

Liberty looked at him, at Latigo, at her father, then at all three of them.

'Men,' she said disgustedly. 'You just can't stand it, can you?'

I could tell by their expressions that they didn't

have any idea what she was talking about.

'Stand what?' her father asked.

'Women doing anything but cooking . . . sewing . . . and having babies.'

'That ain't true,' he argued.

'Oh, isn't it? Then how come you're always hinting that it's time I quit being a deputy marshal and help you raise horses at the ranch?'

'That ain't true, neither. What I said – have said all along – was I wasn't gettin' any younger an' it might be nice, for both of us, if you spent a little more time with me an' quit tryin' to prove you're better than all the other deputies by insistin' on handlin' all the toughest cases.'

'I go where Marshal Macahan sends me. Nothing more.'

'You're forgettin' something, daughter mine. Macahan an' me didn't meet yesterday.'

'Meaning?'

'It was Ezra who brung it up. We were havin' a beer one day in El Paso an' he said he was worried 'bout you maybe gettin' worn down. Said he'd asked you take some time off, time owed you over the years, an' you told him no.'

'He must've had too many beers,' Liberty said, avoiding her father's steady gaze. 'I don't remember having that conversation with him. Ever.'

'Maybe we should ask him together, then,' Drifter said. 'So you can hear it from the horse's mouth.'

Liberty looked at the three men facing her, and

saw nothing but concern for her in their eyes. For some reason that made her even angrier.

'You can all go to hell,' she said. Then to me: 'You'll ride with us till I can think of somewhere safe to leave you.'

'Yes, ma'am,' I said.

'First, though,' she added, 'we've got to find you a horse. Mine's worn out carrying double and I can't risk having him break down.'

CHAPTER EIGHTEEN

Very few of the villagers owned a horse and the two
men who did, refused to sell them. No one was
willing to part with their burros either. Finally, when
it looked liked I was going to have to continue riding
double behind Liberty, Father Ignacio said he knew
of a man who had mules for sale.

'A mule's fine,' Liberty said. 'Take us to him,
padre.'

'Yeah, an' while you're doin' that,' Gabe said,
'me'n Latigo will ask around an' see if anyone has
any guns they want to sell.' They rode off.

Father Ignacio led Liberty, Drifter and me toward
the edge of town. As they walked beside him, and I
brought up the rear with their horses, the padre
warned us that the man we were going to meet was
not clear in the head and that we should not believe
everything he said.

' 'Mean he's *loco*?' Drifter said.

Father Ignacio shrugged his thin, bony shoulders. 'It is not for me to say who is crazy, *señor*. We are all God's children. Only He has the right to judge who we are. All I know is that as a boy, Felipe was taken by *bandidos* and never seen again until a few months ago, when he suddenly showed up and told everyone he had come home to die.'

'What's crazy about that?' Liberty asked. 'Lots of folks come home to die.'

'This is true, *señorita*. And naturally we were all very happy to see one of our own again. But then one day during confession, he begged to be forgiven. When I asked him how he had sinned, he said he did not know because his memory had been taken from him, but that in his mind he saw himself as a drunken *pistolero*, killing men, women and even children. Of course, this is all in his imagination. As you will see for yourselves, he is simply a very old man, now almost blind, whose mind plays tricks on him.'

'As long as he sells us the mule,' Liberty said, 'he can be as crazy as he wants.'

When we reached the old adobe house, the padre led us around in back and there, sitting in the shade, staring blankly out at the flat, empty scrubland, was a tall, gaunt old man dressed like a *campesino*. He had white wavy hair brushed back from his proud, leathery face, a big white mustache and sunken eyes white as milk.

He heard us coming and must have recognized

Father Ignacio's walk because he rose and in Spanish addressed him as padre and bowed politely each time the priest introduced one of us. He then listened as Father Ignacio explained that we had come to buy a mule. Then without a word he walked to a small, mud-walled stable next to the house and went inside.

'He gets around mighty good for a blind man,' Drifter said.

Father Ignacio nodded. 'I once told him the same thing. And he replied that a man cursed by God does not need eyes to see with.'

I didn't understand what he meant. But there was no denying that the old man could move around like he could see.

We heard him talking, too softly to understand what he was saying, and then he came out of the stable. Following him like puppies were two mules. One was gray, like most mules. The other was pure white with pink-red eyes and a stumpy tail. Both mules had bridles but no saddles.

Liberty looked them over and then in Spanish asked the old man how much he wanted for the gray mule.

'The mules are free,' he replied. 'But you must take them both.'

'I only need one – for the young girl, here.'

The old man shrugged. 'I am sorry, *señorita*. They are as two heartbeats: one must follow the other.'

'Judas,' muttered Drifter, 'we don't have time for

this crap.' Then to Liberty: 'Take 'em both. You heard him: they're free.'

Liberty chewed her lip, troubled by something. 'These are fine mules, Old One. Why do you want to give them away?'

'Because wherever you are taking them, *señorita*, this is where I shall die.'

'What's he talking about?' Liberty asked the padre.

Father Ignacio shrugged and pointed to his head, indicating that the old man was *loco*. 'Forgive me,' he said then, 'but I must return to my church.' He hurried off before anyone could stop him.

'Better make up your mind,' Drifter told his daughter. 'We're losin' light fast.'

'All right,' Liberty said to the old man, 'I'll take them both.'

He smiled, like he knew something we didn't, and entered his house.

Just then we heard horses approaching. It was Gabe and Latigo. They dismounted beside us. Latigo still had no six-gun, but he was holding an old, rusty-barreled Mexican army rifle.

'Just pray when I fire this damn' thing,' he said to Liberty, 'that it don't blow up in my face.'

'Like I told him,' Gabe put in, 'I got a Winchester an' a Colt .44 stashed only an hour's ride from here.'

'We don't have an hour to spare,' Liberty said. 'Not if we're going to reach Palomas tonight.'

There was a noise behind us. We all turned,

looked, and saw the old man standing in the doorway of his house. Only now instead of wearing plain white cotton field clothes he was dressed all in black silk. There were silver *conchos* on his sombrero, leather leggings and gun-belt, and a fancy pearl-handled Colt poked out of his tied-down holster. He reminded me of a Mexican *pistolero* I'd seen in this old picture book Ma once showed me.

'What the devil. . . ?' began Liberty.

The old man came toward us, carrying something wrapped in a faded *serape*. He stopped in front of Latigo, smiling as if they were old friends, and said: '*Amigo, me he mantenido estos para usted.*'

'For me?' Latigo said. Puzzled, he looked at Liberty, Drifter and Gabe, adding: 'Why would he keep somethin' for me? I've never seen him afore.'

'Must think you're someone else,' Drifter said.

'See what it is,' Gabe said. 'Don't want to offend the old gent.'

Latigo turned back to the old man. 'Sure you want me to take this?'

'*Sí, señor. Que son tuyas. Solo he side su guardian todos estos anos.*'

Latigo shrugged, took the *serape*, slowly unfolded it to reveal – a gun-belt with two nickel-plated, ivory-grip Colt .44s in the holsters.

Now I was puzzled. If by some chance the guns really were Latigo's, where had the old man gotten them from and why had he been looking after them all these years?

Latigo whistled softly. 'Damn, if I didn't know better, I'd swear this rig was mine.' He drew one of the guns, twirled it on his finger and stuffed it back into the holster. 'Where'd you get these, old man?'

'*No se, señor. No tengo ninguna memoria de ellos.*'

'Says he has no memory of them,' I said as Latigo frowned.

'Well,' Drifter said, indicating the old rifle, ' 'least now you don't have to shoot that rusty ol' sonofabitch!'

'Amen,' Latigo said. Then to the old man: '*Muchas gracias, hombre.* You don't know it, but you may have just won us the war!'

The old man bowed and then said something in Spanish to Latigo.

'This?' Latigo looked at the rusty old rifle in disgust. 'What do you want this old thing for?'

'Just give it to him,' Liberty said before the old man could answer. 'We need to make dust.'

Latigo shrugged and handed the rifle to the old man, '*Aqui. Es tuyo,*' and stepped up into the saddle. Gabe did the same. Liberty said: 'Daddy, help Hope up onto that mule.'

Drifter made a stirrup with his clasped hands and boosted me up onto the back of the gray mule.

At the same time the all-white mule trotted over to the old man and stood patiently next to him, as if it knew what was going to happen.

'Whoa, wait a minute,' Liberty said as the old man used an upturned bucket to help him mount the mule. 'Where d'you think you're going?'

'*A morir,*' he said simply.

CHAPTER NINETEEN

'Says he's going to die,' I told Liberty.

'I heard him,' she said. Then in Spanish she told the old man that she was sorry but he could not go with us, no matter what the reason.

I expected him to argue, to insist on going, but he didn't. He didn't say anything. His expression didn't even change. He just dismounted, sat down on the upturned bucket, rested the old rifle across his lap and went to sleep.

'Let's go,' Liberty said. She tapped the bay with her spurs and the four of them rode off. I tried to follow them but the gray mule wouldn't move. I kicked it and yelled at it and whipped it with the reins. It didn't matter. Nothing could make that mule move.

Latigo, Drifter and Gabe reined up while Liberty swung her horse around and rode back to me. 'What's wrong?'

'It won't giddyup,' I said.

Liberty did her best to make the mule move. So did Drifter, who rode back beside us. But it was useless. It just stood there like a statue.

'Try the other one,' Drifter said. He grabbed me around the waist, rode alongside the all-white mule and swung me over onto its back.

But it was as stubborn as the gray mule.

Angry and frustrated, Liberty rode up to the old man and told him that if he didn't order the mules to move, she'd shoot them.

The old man spoke without opening his milky white eyes.

'He says,' I began.

'That they will only move if he goes – yeah, I heard him.'

'Forget the goddamn mules,' Drifter said. 'Hope can ride behind me.'

'No,' Liberty said. 'Like I said before, we can't afford to have one of the horses break down.' She sighed wearily. Then she told the old man that she had changed her mind. He could accompany us, but only as far as Palomas. Then he was on his own. Her Spanish was a bit rusty and twice I had to correct her when she used the wrong word. 'And tell him this,' she added to me. 'If he falls off or gets lost along the way because he can't see, that's on him. We're not stopping for any reason. And make that very clear, scout – not for *any* reason!'

I repeated what Liberty had said to the old man. He nodded politely, rose and got up on the bucket again. He made no signal but the white mule trotted over and stood beside him. The old man whispered something to it and climbed onto its back.

Liberty and the others turned their horses around and rode out into the desert. And just like that, the mules followed.

He was some old blind man.

I had never been to Palomas. But according to Gabe, who often went there, it wasn't much more than an hour's ride.

We rode in silence. Liberty set the pace, an easy loping gait that the mules were able to keep up with, and soon the miles were falling behind us. Darkness came. Drifting clouds hid the moon and the stars and it became difficult to see more than a short distance in any direction. Worried that one of the horses might step into a rut or hole and break its leg, Liberty slowed the pace. But shortly the clouds thinned out, letting the moon peek through, and now I could see not only the flat scrub-covered desert but also some distant round hills and beyond the hills, so far-off they were tiny, the snowy jagged peaks of the Sierra Madre Occidental.

Liberty picked up the pace again and I heard Gabe, who was riding behind her and Drifter, tell Latigo that another ten minutes or so would bring us to the outskirts of Palomas.

'*Nos acercamos a Palomas, señor,*' I told the old man.

'*Sí, lo se, poco uno,*' he said.

112

Wondering how he could know if he was blind, I decided to test him. Pointing ahead, I asked him if he could see the mountains in the distance.

He didn't answer for a few moments and I wondered if he'd heard me. Then he raised his hand, held it a few inches from his face and told me that all he could see was a blurred outline of his fingers.

It didn't make sense but I was too polite to tell him. We rode on in silence save for the yelping of the coyotes as they talked to each other.

Then in the distance I could see the glow of cantina lights.

The old man must have seen them too because he crossed himself and murmured: '*Pronto me descanse en paz.*'

I knew then what he'd meant by a man cursed by God does not need eyes to see with. At the same time I wondered how he expected to rest in peace if he'd been cursed by God. It was all very puzzling.

CHAPTER TWENTY

As we approached the outskirts we could hear cantina music and random shots being fired, followed by loud, drunken laughter. Liberty reined up and signaled for everyone to dismount behind some large boulders.

Gathering us together in a circle she took a Wanted posted from her pocket, unfolded it to show the faces of the two escaped convicts, Coyle Dano and Heck Canfield. 'You ever seen these two before?' she asked Drifter and Gabe. Then as they shook their heads: 'Is there any possibility they could have run into you anywhere?'

'Not me,' Gabe said.

'Me neither,' Drifter said.

'You're sure? Think now. We can't afford to make a mistake. We lose the element of surprise, we're in deep trouble.'

'Positive,' Drifter said. Gabe nodded in agreement.

'OK,' Liberty continued, 'this is what I want you to do: Ride in ahead of us. Find out exactly where they are, how many men they've got, and, if they're holed up in one of the cantinas, how drunk they are.'

'And if they got the Gardner machine gun yet,' added Latigo.

'Anythin' else?' Drifter asked Liberty.

'Can I say something?' I interrupted.

'Go ahead, scout.'

'If I show you what Aunt Connie looks like, will you try to find out if she's still alive?'

'You have a picture of her?' Liberty asked.

I nodded. While they'd been talking I'd quickly drawn her face in my little sketchpad. I tore out the page and gave it to Drifter, saying: 'I've signed it. That way, if you talk to her, she'll know we're friends.'

Drifter nodded, 'Do what I can,' tucked the picture into his pocket and turned back to Liberty. 'Be back soon.'

Liberty took out a man's silver fob watch from her jeans, opened it so the dial showed and held it up to her father. 'You got an hour. After that, I'll figure something went wrong and come in after you.'

Drifter, who'd been looking at the watch as if he couldn't believe what he was seeing, now said: 'Where'd you find that?'

'Momma's jewelry box.'

'When?'

'That first time we rode out to the ranch after I came home from school. I was in the bedroom, poking around in the ashes. I recognized little scraps of her clothes and keepsakes – you know how she could never throw anything away – and there was the watch. Guess for some odd reason it didn't get burned up in the fire. . . .'

'All these years,' Drifter said, sounding hurt. 'Why didn't you say somethin'?'

Liberty shrugged. 'I don't know.' She guiltily avoided his gaze. 'I should have, I know. Sorry.'

Drifter nodded, sighed and gave a sad little smile.

'When did you give it to her?' Liberty asked.

'Day after you were born. Belonged to my father. An' his father before him. I snagged it day after he passed. Figured if I didn't the lawyers would take it to help pay off some of his debts.'

Liberty toed the ground with her boot. 'I'm really sorry, Daddy. I should've told you.'

Drifter studied her for a moment then cupped his hands about her face and gently kissed her on the forehead.

A distant coyote yip-yipped at the moon.

'Reckon we should be movin' out,' Gabe said.

'An hour,' Liberty repeated to Drifter.

Her father nodded. He and Gabe went to their horses. The all-black stallion took a swipe at Gabe as he mounted. He jumped back, cursing.

Latigo shook his head, puzzled. '*Amigo*, you're a hard man to figure.'

'Yeah?' Gabe said. 'Why's that?'

'Well, most folks are smart enough not to make

the same mistake twice. You, now, long as I've known you, you've always cottoned to black horses that bite. Why is that, you think?'

'They remind me of Brandy,' Gabe said. 'Mean as that Morgan was, I always had a soft spot for the ornery sonofabitch.'

Latigo chuckled. 'One day, *amigo*, that soft spot's goin' to be the death of you.'

'That's why I got you,' Gabe said, chuckling, 'To watch my back.' He stepped up into the saddle, swung his horse around and joined Drifter, who was already mounted.

'Back soon,' Drifter told Liberty. He and Gabe spurred their horses in the direction of town.

Liberty looked after her father. 'Be safe,' she whispered.

I took out my little sketchpad and pencil. 'Mind if I draw a picture of you?' I said.

'What? Oh-h, sure. If you want to.'

'Over there,' I said. I pointed at a flat rock where the old man was sitting, smoking a thin Mexican cigar. 'Next to him.'

'All right,' she said. 'But make it quick.'

An hour passed. Then another ten minutes. Liberty kept looking at her watch and then at the town, her frown darkening as each minute passed.

'Five more minutes,' she told Latigo. 'Then we go in, regardless.'

'Relax,' he said, thumbing off. 'There they are now.'

Dismounting, Drifter and Gabe loosened the cinches on their horses and then joined Liberty and Latigo. I sat on the flat rock beside the old man, listening to what they had to say.

'They're there, both of 'em,' Drifter said, 'in a cantina called El Tecolote.'

' 'Long with twelve hard cases mean enough to eat sand an' rape their sisters,' Gabe added.

'Save the dime novel descriptions,' Liberty said after a quick glance at me. 'Just tell me what I need to know, dammit.'

'Easy. Don't throw a hitch,' her father said. 'Turns out, it's better than we thought.'

'Go on.'

'Half of 'em are skunked, the others well on their way.'

'That include Dano and Canfield?'

'No. They'd been drinkin', but mostly they had their minds locked on other things.' He, like Liberty, threw a glance my way before adding: 'Last we saw 'em they were headed into a back room with two tamales.'

'Was one of them Aunt Connie?' I said, knowing I'd most likely get yelled at for interrupting.

'No,' Drifter said. 'We never caught so much as a glimpse of your aunt all the time we were in Palomas.'

'Don't worry,' Liberty said, seeing my long face. 'Just because they didn't see her, doesn't mean any harm's come to her.'

'That's right,' Gabe assured me. 'Truth is, missy, your aunt's probably locked up in a room somewhere. An' once the gunplay's over, an' the marshal here's got her prisoners, we'll find that room, an' your aunt, then you two can return home safe'n sound.'

I knew he was trying to make me feel better, so I nodded and said no more.

'Let's get back to Palomas,' Liberty said, turning to Drifter and Gabe. 'This back room you say Dano and Canfield went into with the women – did it have a window?'

'Can't rightly say,' Drifter said. 'We couldn't get close enough to see without tippin' our hand.'

She looked concerned. 'I need to know that before we hit them. I don't want them skipping out a window, not when we're so close to taking them.'

'There's a narrow alley behind the cantina,' Gabe said, 'runs right past the room an' the rear entrance. I'll be in it when you three bust in the front door.'

'No,' Latigo said. 'I was the one them bastards staked out over the ants. Wouldn't cheat me out of a chance for payback, would you, *amigo*?'

'Fair enough,' Liberty said. 'But if there's no window, don't be too long about finding that back door. We're going to be hard-pressed to handle twelve guns, drunk or sober.'

'You're readin' my mind,' Drifter said. He went to his horse and took something from the saddle-bag.

'Where the hell'd you get those?' Liberty

exclaimed as she saw he was holding several sticks of dynamite.'

'Courtesy of the US Army.'

'Dano or Canfield or their men must've ambushed some soldiers 'cross the border,' Gabe said.

'How do you know that?' Liberty asked.

' 'Cause there was a freight wagon tied up in front of the cantina,' Drifter said. 'Had US Army stamped on its sides—'

'An' was loaded down with kegs of gunpowder, boxes of dynamite an' ammo,' Gabe added.

'So we helped ourselves to a few sticks,' Drifter said. 'You know, to even up the odds a little.'

'What 'bout the Gardner gun?' Latigo said.

'Ain't arrived yet,' Gabe said. Then to Liberty: 'I know you're ramroddin' this outfit but if you want my advice, it's time to tell the bugler to blow charge.'

CHAPTER
TWENTY-ONE

While they were talking, I sat on the rock next to the old man, wondering what Liberty planned to do with me. I didn't have long to wait. Shortly, she left Drifter, Gabe and Latigo and came over to me.

'Get mounted,' she said. 'We're leaving. No, not you, *señor*,' she added as the old man, seeing me get up, also rose. 'This is where we part company.'

She'd spoken to him in Spanish. The old man looked at her, his face as blank as his milky white eyes, and replied in perfect English: 'It is God's wish that I protect the young girl. To do this, Marshal, I must be permitted to go wherever she goes.'

I gaped at him. So did Liberty. Behind her Drifter, Gabe and Latigo stopped talking and joined us.

'Why didn't you tell us you spoke English?' Drifter growled at him.

'You did not ask me,' replied the old man. 'You were too busy being condescending – treating me like a helpless old blind man.'

'You are a helpless old blind man,' said Liberty, finding her voice.

The old man smiled, like he knew a secret, and removed his black sombrero. His wrinkled fingers felt each of the silver *conchos* adorning the hatband until he found one that was loose. Jerking it free, he tossed it into the moonlit darkness. I heard it clink as it hit a rock, then silence.

The old man drew and fired his Colt at the sound. He only fired once then holstered the six-gun as smoothly as he'd drawn it.

'If you would be so kind,' he said to me, 'as to bring it to me.'

I looked at Liberty. She nodded. I ran off in the direction of where I had heard the *concho* hitting the rock. I searched in an ever-widening circle. It took a few minutes then I saw the *concho* glinting on the moon-whitened sand to my left. Picking it up, I looked at it and saw it was bent as if hit by something hard: like a bullet.

Wondering how the old man had done it, I ran back to Liberty. 'He hit it,' I said, handing her the *concho*.

'It bounced off a rock,' Latigo reminded.

Liberty showed him the bent *concho*. 'A rock didn't do this,' she said. There was new respect in her voice. To the old man, she added: 'Tell me, *señor*. Why do you believe it is God's wish that you protect Hope?'

'Because it is written in my mind.'

'That's gibberish,' Drifter said.

Liberty silenced him with a look. 'How is that possible,' she said to the old man, 'considering you didn't even know Hope, or any of us existed until a few hours ago?'

The old man's mind seemed to wander for a few moments before he said: 'It was never my wish to return to the village of my birth. Yet return I did. I knew then it must be for a purpose. I waited and waited for that purpose to be made clear to me. It never was. Then you came to buy one of my mules for the young girl and suddenly I knew I'd found my purpose.'

Liberty silently chewed on the old man's words. I watched her. No one can tell what another person is thinking, but I sensed that unlike Gabe, Drifter and Latigo, she believed the old man, as I did; and at that moment I learned something important from her: trust your instincts, your gut feelings, as Pa called it, and don't let other people sway your thinking.

Liberty, having made her mind up, said: 'One last question, Old One. When you fired and hit the *concho* – was that blind luck?'

'I will do it again if you wish, Marshal.'

Liberty shook her head. 'That won't be necessary.'

'Then you will permit me to protect the young one?'

'Yes. Have you been here before,' she asked, 'to

Palomas, I mean?'

'Many times – though not recently.'

Liberty looked at Drifter, Gabe and Latigo. She was fully in charge now and when she spoke, it was like a general talking to her troops. 'I need someplace for him to hole up with Hope until the shooting's over. You three know the town – any ideas?'

'There's an old hotel at the far end of town,' Gabe said. 'Hotel Cielo. The tamales takes special customers there an'—'

'Skip the cheap details,' she barked. 'Is it safe?'

'As any other place in Palomas, yeah.'

'I know of this hotel,' the old man said as Liberty turned back to him. 'Is this where you wish us to go?'

Liberty hesitated, looked at me, at her father, at Gabe and Latigo and then back at the old man. 'Yes.' To me she said: 'I'm going to ask you to grow up fast. Be an adult.'

'I will,' I promised. 'What do you want me to do?'

'Give me your word that you will not leave the hotel until I come for you.'

'I won't,' I said.

'Under any circumstances.'

'Promise.'

'Very well. Then you and Señor—' She paused as she realized something, then said: 'I don't know your name, *señor*.'

He hesitated. I could tell he didn't want to reveal his name. 'Don Rojo,' he said reluctantly.

'Well, Don Rojo, I—'

'Hold on,' Gabe said suddenly. Then to the old man: 'You're Rojo?'

'*Sí, señor.*'

'Juan Manuel Rojo – the man they call *El Muerto*?'

'There are some who once called me that, *sí*.'

'Well, I'll be damned,' Gabe said. He turned to Liberty, adding: 'Might want to reconsider, Emily. Back in his day, this old man was a stone-cold killer – a Mexican gun for hire. Gunned down fifty people, maybe more—'

'Señor,' the old man protested, 'that is all in the past. I have not even worn a gun, let alone fired one, in more than twenty years.'

Latigo thumbed at the bent *concho* in Liberty's hand. 'Seems like you ain't lost your touch, *amigo*.'

'A caged bird does not forget how to fly, *señor*.'

'Caged birds don't drink tequila,' Drifter said, 'or become trigger-happy killers when they do.' Then to Liberty: 'Sober he was a ruthless, deadly gunman; drunk, he was worse.'

The old man looked ashamed but did not defend himself.

I looked at Liberty. She was silently raging. I knew she was about to get rid of the old man. I didn't want that. At that moment I didn't care how many people he'd killed. I felt safe with him and sensed he would protect me with his life.

'I'll go with him,' I said, as if my opinion mattered. 'Don Rojo won't hurt me.'

'No,' Liberty said. 'I can't risk it.'

'Please,' I begged. 'I'll be all right. I know I will.'

The old man turned his blind eyes to Liberty: 'As a young man, Father Ignacio went to prison for stealing a horse. Yet now he is a priest, a man of God – is it not possible that I could change also?'

His plea stabbed Liberty. Undecided, she looked at her father as if for advice; then, before he could give her any, said to the old man: 'Father Ignacio told me you'd lost your memory, but that you had nightmares in which you saw yourself killing men, women and even children. He didn't believe you. Said it was all in your imagination. Now Gabe, here, says it's true. Is it?'

The old man nodded sadly.

'Hope is a child – how can you expect me to believe you won't harm her?'

'I am a different man now.'

'That's not enough reason.'

'There are not answers for everything,' the old man said.

'How about losing your memory – is that true or did you lie about that too?'

'It is the truth.'

'Yet you can remember your name? Why is that?'

'Occasionally, glimpses of my past return. As for now,' he said regretfully, 'it is well known that mothers still frighten their children just by saying my name. Worse, once people learn who I am – was, I'm forced to move on. I am a man without a hope or dignity. It is a curse – a well-deserved curse that I must live with until the Devil calls me to hell.'

Liberty absorbed his words and then looked at me. 'Not too late to change your mind, scout.'

I shook my head. 'I trust him,' I said. 'I know he'll look after me.'

Liberty released all her frustration in a long, weary sigh. 'All right,' she said, including everyone. 'We'll stick to the plan. Get mounted.' To me she added: 'I wish there was another way to do this, scout, but for the life of me I can't think of one.'

'It's all right,' I said. 'I'll be fine. Honest.'

Liberty smiled and ruffled my hair. 'Know what? I have a feeling we're going to be friends forever.'

'I hope so.'

'I know so.' She hugged me, so tight I could barely breathe, and then helped me up onto the gray mule. She then looked at the old man who was already astride the white mule and said: 'Guard her with your life, Don Rojo.'

'I will,' he assured her. 'Come,' he said to me. 'It is time to ride.'

The two of us urged the mules forward and rode on into town. I looked back once. Liberty was now mounted on the bay, watching us. She looked strong, proud and confident, as if nothing could go wrong. When I grow up, I thought, I want to be just like her – only as a painter, of course.

I faced front. I heard her voice telling Drifter, Gabe and Latigo to split up and ride into Palomas separately. Then we were hidden from her by the outlying houses and I tried not to worry about what would happen to me next.

CHAPTER TWENTY-TWO

Because the Hotel Cielo was on the other side of town, the old man and I kept to the outskirts and entered from the west. Even in the dark the hotel was not hard to find. An old two-story, whitewashed adobe building with outside stairs leading to the upper rooms, it stood at the end of the main street, at an inward angle so that its windows faced east.

Our room overlooked the street. It was no bigger than my bedroom at home. It had pale ochre walls and a ceiling that needed painting. There was a small iron bed, a chair, and a chest of drawers with a pitcher of water and a chipped porcelain basin on top of it. It had no bathroom, which was down the hall, and there were no pictures on the walls. But it did have a window. Opening it, I looked out and realized I could see the cantina, *El Tecolote*.

It was on the other side of the dirt street, about

fifteen buildings away. Out front two bearded gunmen stood leaned against a freight wagon. The back of it was covered by a tarp, but I could see the outline of kegs and crates piled underneath it and guessed this was the wagon Drifter talked about – the one filled with gunpowder, dynamite and ammunition that had been stolen from a US Army post. There were no street lights, like there are now in Santa Rosa, but the moon was bright and the lights in the windows of other cantinas and stores enabled me to see everything that was going on.

I pulled Don Rojo to the window and told him what I saw. 'From here,' I said, forgetting he was blind, 'we can watch what happens.'

'It is not safe,' he said. 'You will sit on the bed till it is over.'

'But if I don't watch,' I argued, 'how are we going to know what happens?'

'The marshal will tell us when she comes for you.'

'If she's wounded, she can't come,' I said darkly, 'and I won't know if she's wounded, or if Gabe or Drifter or Latigo are wounded either, unless I watch.'

'It is not for you to argue, child.' Don Rojo closed the window and went and sat down on the wooden chair.

'I ain't a child,' I blurted, forgetting my promise to Ma to always speak like a lady. 'And you ain't my father. You can't tell me what to do. If I want to look out the window, I will!'

He looked at me with his milky white eyes, his

lined, gaunt face filled with concern, and said quietly: 'I have given my word to protect you. I cannot do this if you will not obey me.'

I immediately felt bad for shouting at him. 'Listen,' I said, 'what if I don't open the window but just stand there, you know, to one side, and watch? Would that be all right?'

'It would be safer,' he conceded.

I stood on the right side of the window, with my shoulder flattened against the wall, and looked out along the street at the cantina. Several horses were tied up outside. Mexican music and loud laughter came from inside. Occasionally drunks came staggering out. Some had women with them; others just fired their guns in the air and then, laughing and slapping each other on the back, lurched across the street to one of the other cantinas.

As I watched, Liberty and Drifter rode up, approaching from different directions. Pretending not to know one another, they dismounted and tied their horses to the hitch-rail outside the livery stable that was several doors down from *El Tecolote*. They stood there, next to their horses, casually looking around, and then pulled out their rifles. Drifter lit a cigar and puffed on it to make sure it was burning well. Then, making sure that no one was watching, he grabbed the sticks of dynamite from his saddlebag and quickly stuffed them into his pants under his jacket.

Shortly, Gabe rode up. Ignoring Liberty and

Drifter, he dismounted and tied up alongside them. Almost immediately, Latigo came out of a side street. He paid no attention to Liberty or the others, but rode into a nearby alley, on around behind the cantina.

Liberty levered a round into her Winchester then looked at the two bearded men leaned against the freight wagon. Both were more interested in what was going on inside the cantina than guarding the wagon. Their backs were turned toward Liberty. She looked at Drifter and nodded. Then she nodded at Gabe. Both men swung in behind her as she walked toward the freight wagon.

I closed my eyes and said a little prayer asking God to keep them all safe. It only took a moment. When I opened my eyes they were only a few steps from the guards. I watched, nervously twisting my braids around my fingers, as Liberty stopped in front of them. She said something and pointed off. The guards turned their heads, looking in the direction she was pointing.

Immediately, Drifter and Gabe closed in and slammed them across the back of the head with their rifles. The guards dropped soundlessly where they stood. Drifter and Gabe dragged them into the alley separating the cantina from the general store, while Liberty quickly climbed up on the wagon seat, grabbed the reins and slapped the team with them. The four horses lunged forward, pulling the heavy wagon slowly on down the street.

Drifter and Gabe jogged along behind it, now and then looking back to see if they were being followed. They weren't. Shortly, they turned into an alley and I lost sight of them.

I turned away from the window and told the old man what I'd seen.

He smiled, pleased. '*Bueno*,' he said. 'The plan, it goes well.'

I turned back to the window. Nothing unusual was happening on the street. I flattened myself against the wall in order to see all the way down the street in case Liberty or Drifter and Gabe were coming back. They weren't.

It was then I saw three drunks stagger out of the cantina opposite *El Tecolote*. They were laughing and dragging a woman with them. I didn't see her face but her clothes were torn and dirty and her dark hair all messy. She was fighting them, trying to get away. But even drunk they were too strong for her. They hit her, sending her sprawling, and while two of them held her down the other one ripped her blouse off, baring her breasts.

I wished I had a gun so I could shoot them.

The three drunks laughed even harder. Two of them started fighting over a bottle of tequila one was holding. As they tried to push each other away and take a swig, the woman twisted loose and kicked the man who'd torn her blouse off between the legs. He yowled and doubled over. The other two men tried to grab her but the woman was too quick for them. She grabbed two handfuls of dirt and threw it in their faces. As they staggered back, pawing at their eyes, the woman snatched the bottle away from the man holding it and broke it over the head of the man she'd kicked. He went down and sat there in the dirt, stunned, blood running down his face.

The woman bolted. As she came running up the street, hair flying, arms crossed in an effort to cover her breasts, two of the men angrily stumbled after her.

I watched her, praying that they wouldn't catch her.

But prayers don't always work. Another man, most likely a friend of the men chasing her, stepped out from behind a wagon and tripped her. She went sprawling. The man grasped her by the hair and held her, struggling, until the other men came running up.

They dragged her to her feet and held her, while the man she'd hit with the bottle staggered up. He pulled a knife, pressed it against her throat and said something threatening.

She spat in his face.

Enraged, the man slashed her throat with the knife.

The men holding her let her go and she stumbled back and sank to her knees. She grasped her throat with both hands, trying to stop the bleeding. But it was useless and she slowly collapsed on her back, dying.

It was then I saw her face.
It was Aunt Connie!

CHAPTER TWENTY-THREE

I don't remember how I got out into the street.

What I *do* remember is kneeling beside Aunt Connie, desperately trying to stop the blood spurting from the gash in her throat. But no matter how hard I pressed my hands over the wound, the blood continued to seep between my fingers and slowly all the life went out of my her big dark eyes.

'P-Please don't die,' I begged her. 'Please . . . Aunt Connie . . . please don't die. . . .'

But she died anyway.

I don't know if she recognized me before she died, or if she even saw me at all. I was hoping she did, but she didn't show it. Her eyes went glassy and I knew she was dead.

I was crying by then. I looked up and through my tears saw the men – four of them now – staggering along the street in the direction of the cantina. Their backs were turned toward me but I could hear them laughing. I wanted to kill them . . . all of them . . . slowly, over a fire, like the Mescaleros used to do to their prisoners when Pa was my age. But what could I do? I didn't even have a gun. Just then one of the men hurled the empty tequila bottle high in the air while the others shot at it, missing in their drunkenness. It gave me an idea. Maybe if I followed them, got close enough and waited until they were drunk, I could grab one of their guns and shoot them. I stood up, ready to run after them.

Someone behind me grasped my arm, stopping me. Startled, I screamed and struggled to break loose. I was crying so hard, I could barely see who was holding me. But as he started talking to me, his voice soothing and calming, I realized it was the old man, Don Rojo.

I was so relieved I threw my arms around him and sobbed against his chest. He stroked my hair and continued to try and calm me. Between sobs I pointed at my aunt's corpse and blurted out what happened. I then pointed down the street at the four men, screaming out that they had killed her. They must have heard me, because they stopped, turned and looked back at me. One of them said something and the others nodded.

They started back toward me.

I panicked. 'They're coming!' I cried to the old man.

'I see them,' he said. He spoke quietly, calmly,

without fear, and gently pushed me behind him. Then he turned and faced the four men and without looking back at me, said: 'Run, Little One. Go hide!'

When I didn't move, he repeated himself.

'Come with me,' I begged, tugging on his arm.

'Would you have me break my word?'

'But they'll kill you.'

'It is time,' he said. Then he said: '*Vaya, por favor.*'

I ran.

I didn't go far. There was a narrow walkway between the hotel and the next building. I ducked down it, then peered around the side of the hotel and watched as the four men fanned out in front of the old man.

Don Rojo didn't move. His milky white eyes stared at the men.

They stopped about ten yards from him, laughing, taunting him, describing how they were going to shoot him to pieces and then feed the pieces to the dogs. 'An' after we're done with you, old man,' one of the men said, 'we're gonna find your gran'-daughter ... maybe have ourselves some fun with her.'

Those were his last words.

Don Rojo drew his Colt and fired, the bullet punching a hole in the man's forehead. He stood there a moment, eyes wide with surprise, as if unable to believe he was dead, and then collapsed.

For an instant the other men stared at the corpse,

shocked.

In that instant Don Rojo fanned his Colt. He fired so quickly, the five shots made only one continuous roar. The three men in front of him staggered back, blood welling from their wounds. One died instantly. The other two managed to drag out their guns and get off several shots – before crumpling to the street.

The tall, gaunt old man remained standing. Calmly, he broke out the cylinder of his Colt and reached for a cartridge in his gun-belt. For a moment I thought he hadn't been hit. But even as he pulled a cartridge from his belt, he stiffened and swayed unsteadily. The cartridge dropped from his wrinkled fingers and landed at his feet. He dropped the Colt back into the holster, turned and looked at me – as if he'd known all along where I was hiding.

'You are not hurt?' he asked as I ran up to him.

'N-No. I'm fine.'

'*Bueno.*' He stared at me with those sightless, milky white eyes. Always before I thought they were ugly. But now, as I looked into them, I saw they were filled with warmth and compassion.

'Do not remember me unkindly,' he said softly.

I started to say I wouldn't . . . but before I could get the words out, he crumpled and collapsed at my feet.

I knew he was dead before I knelt and touched him.

I started to say a prayer over him – then stopped, startled, as there was a huge, thunderous explosion farther along the street.

CHAPTER TWENTY-FOUR

I looked toward the cantina, expecting to see it in flames. But the explosion was a short distance beyond it. Flaming debris hurtled skyward and then rained down on the surrounding rooftops.

Everyone came stumbling out of the *El Tecolote*, as well as all the other cantinas facing the street. Many of them were heavily armed gunmen, weapons in hand, ready to shoot anything threatening. Most were half-drunk and stood there in the street, swaying, looking around as they tried to figure out what had caused the explosion.

Among the gunmen outside *El Tecolote* stood two men I recognized – the escaped convicts Liberty was after. Their hair was longer and they looked older and grubbier than their pictures on the Wanted posters, but there was no mistaking who it was.

They were yelling at the gunmen around them. I

couldn't hear what they were saying because everyone else in the street was shouting as well. But they kept pointing at the spot where the freight wagon had been standing and were obviously enraged that it was missing. Just then the two men who'd been guarding the wagon came stumbling out of the alley, each one clasping the back of his head.

Dano gave an order to the gunmen, who grabbed the two guards and dragged them before him. The guards tried to explain what had happened, but before they could finish Dano jerked his iron and gunned them both down.

It was then I saw Latigo step out of the cantina. He was empty-handed but around his waist was the gunbelt with the ivory-handled Colts that Don Rojo had kept for him. Pausing a short distance behind Dano and Canfield, he signaled to someone across the street.

I looked and saw Liberty and Drifter, rifles in hand, crouched behind a wagon. Liberty waved back in response, said something to her father then stood up and fired a shot in the air.

Everyone on the street froze and looked at Liberty.

She stepped forward, her rifle aimed at Dano and Canfield.

Drifter followed her, a few steps to her left.

As I wondered where Gabe was, I saw him step out from a nearby doorway and quickly join Liberty and Drifter. His Winchester rested in the crook of his arm.

As the three of them walked grimly across the street, men and women in their way quickly stepped aside, leaving them a clear path to Dano and Canfield and the gunmen flanking them.

If Liberty realized they were out-gunned by at least four to one, she never showed it. She walked as tall and straight and bobcat-easy as the first time I saw her, when she stepped out of the mesquite on our ranch. I doubted if I would ever again see her as brave and fearless as she looked right now, and I wanted to take out my little sketchpad and draw her so I'd never forget, but I was afraid I might miss something.

Liberty stopped a few feet in front of Dano and Canfield, Drifter and Gabe pulling up alongside her.

'I'm Deputy US Marshal Mercer,' she said, pinning her star on her jacket. 'Drop your gun-belts. You're under arrest.'

Dano and Canfield looked at her, unable to believe her gall.

No one on the street moved or made a sound.

Then Dano and Canfield exploded into laughter. It was loud, mocking laughter and pretty soon the drunken gunmen around them joined in.

'That star don't mean dog-squat down here,' Dano said.

'As for arrestin' us, girlie,' Canfield said, amused, 'whyn't you go ahead an' try. Hell, I ain't shot a Federal Marshal all week!'

The gunmen howled. So did some of the onlookers.

Even Liberty was amused enough to give a slight smile. 'Maybe you're right,' she conceded. 'Maybe trying to arrest you *is* a waste of time—'

'Damn' straight,' Canfield said. 'So why don't you get rid of that star, girlie, then you an' me will grab us a bottle an' go someplace where we can have ourselves some fun?'

'I've got a better idea,' Liberty said. She reached out to Drifter, who took one of the sticks of dynamite from his pants, lit the fuse with his cigar and handed it to Liberty. 'Why don't I just blow us all to hell?'

She dropped the burning stick of dynamite on the ground between them and smiled mockingly at them.

Alarmed, the gunmen around the two convicts backed up – while behind them everyone in the street scattered in panic.

'Don't sweat it, boys,' Canfield told his men. 'She's runnin a bluff.'

'Could be he's right,' Liberty admitted. 'I mean, why would I or my deputies want to cash in our chips for gutless, murdering trash like your bosses, here? It doesn't make sense. 'Course,' she added after a pause, 'my being a woman and everything, you have to ask yourselves if I've *got* any sense. . . .'

As she was talking the fuse kept burning lower and lower.

Finally, it was too much for the gunmen. They fled, disappearing into alleys and side streets alongside the nearest buildings.

'Well, now,' Liberty said, smiling at the two heavily sweating convicts, 'seems your men aren't loyal enough to stick around and find out.'

Canfield and Dano didn't say anything. They stood there, teeth gritted, eyes fixed on the burning dynamite for another long moment. Then Dano cracked, and stepping forward went to stamp out the fuse.

There was a shot.

For a moment I wasn't sure who'd fired it because I hadn't seen anyone move. Then I saw the nickel-plated Colt. 44 in Latigo's left hand and realized he'd drawn and fired so quickly, I'd missed it.

Dano lay writhing on the ground, blood coming from a hole in his boot.

The dynamite continued to burn.

'You hog-suckin' miserable bitch,' began Canfield.

Latigo went to shoot him but Liberty raised her hand, stopping him.

She then jerked her iron and fired, clipping off the burning fuse a moment before it ignited the dynamite. In almost the same smooth motion, she holstered her gun and faced Canfield.

'All right,' she told him, as calmly as if she were borrowing a cup of sugar, 'unbuckle your gun-belt and turn around.'

'You ain't gonna live long enough to see me do that,' Canfield said.

'Wrong,' Liberty replied. 'I'm going to live long enough to take you back to Huntsville and see you hang.'

'Reckon we'll end it here an' now, then.'

'You call it,' Liberty said quietly.

'Sure, easy for you to crowd me,' Canfield sneered, 'when you got three deputies backin' you up.'

Liberty's gold-brown eyes narrowed and took on a look that I knew meant the end for Canfield. Without turning, she spoke to Drifter, Latigo and Gabe: 'This is between him and me,' she said, her voice barely more than a whisper. 'No one else.'

'Emily, you don't have to do this,' her father said.

'Yes,' she said. 'As a matter of fact, I do.'

While she was talking Canfield went for his gun.

Liberty's right hand blurred. Her Colt .45, the same gun that had once belonged to another Deputy US Marshal named Liberty, leaped into her hand and spoke justice.

Two guns roared as one. I closed my eyes, not wanting to see what I almost knew would happen – that the only woman who could even come close to taking Ma's place would be lying dead in the street.

CHAPTER TWENTY-FIVE

Once the roar of the guns faded, I heard a body thump to the ground. I desperately wanted to see who it was but I dreaded opening my eyes. With Liberty dead, I had no one.

A long silence followed. Nothing stirred. My heart threatened to pound through my chest. I wanted to pray, to ask God to please let Liberty be the one still standing, but what was the point? I'd prayed for Ma not to die; I prayed for Pa not to die; and both of them had died. Obviously, God wasn't listening to me.

Then, as if from afar, like birds chirping at dawn, voices all along the street began talking as everyone emerged from their hiding places.

I forced myself to open my eyes. The first thing I saw was Drifter, Latigo and Gabe all gathered around someone kneeling beside a corpse. For one awful moment I couldn't see if it was Liberty or Canfield. Then they stepped back to give the person room to stand – and I saw it was Liberty.

Relief washed through me. I ran toward her, calling her name. She didn't hear me at first, but as I got closer she turned and saw me. She smiled and waved and opened her arms to hug me. I jumped into them and hugged her back. It was the happiest I'd been since Ma passed.

'Where's the old man?' she asked, putting me down.

'Dead,' I said, thumbing toward his corpse that still lay in the street in front of the four dead men. 'I was looking out the window and saw this man kill my aunt and . . . and . . . I ran out into the street to—'

'Wait, wait,' Liberty said. 'Your aunt's dead?'

'Yes. This man had a knife and . . . and. . . .' I couldn't finish.

'Damn . . .' Liberty put her arm around me. 'I'm so sorry, scout—'

At that moment, behind her, Latigo and Gabe dragged Dano to his feet. Blood was leaking out of the bullet hole in his boot. He cursed them and pulled away, tried to put his weight on his wounded foot. The pain made him grunt. Grimacing, he hobbled forward – at the same time pulling a two-shot derringer from his jacket sleeve. He aimed it at Latigo, who had half-turned away, and fired. The bullet struck Latigo in the shoulder, rendering it useless. The little Texan stumbled back and before either Gabe or Drifter could grab Dano, he fired again. The slug ripped through Gabe's left arm, spinning him around.

Dano threw the derringer at Drifter and started hobbling away. But he hadn't taken more than two steps when Drifter fired his Winchester from the hip. Dano pitched forward onto his face, dead before he hit the dirt.

Liberty spun around and hurried to Latigo's side.

'You all right?' she asked him. There was deep concern in her voice and I suddenly realized as much as she didn't want to, she still loved him.

'Just winged,' he lied. He looked bitterly at Dano's corpse, adding: 'No dinky little woman's gun is goin' to put an end to me.'

'How 'bout you?' Drifter asked Gabe, whose shirt-sleeve was stained red.

'I'll live,' he said. He looked at the sullen faces gathered around them, some of which belonged to the gunmen who'd fled from the burning dynamite. 'But I reckon it's time to burn daylight.'

Liberty nodded in agreement. 'Start for the horses. But do it nice and easy, so they don't think we're running scared.'

'Let's not give 'em a chance to shoot us in the back, either,' added Drifter. 'Keep the bastards in front of you.' He levered another round into his Winchester and trained it on the angry mob. Latigo and Gabe did the same thing; while Liberty, one hand grasping mine, the other holding her Colt, slowly began to back up to the horses tied up by the livery stable.

The gunmen started inching forward. I could see the hate in their fierce dark eyes and knew they were itching to shoot us.

Then a strange thing happened. A boy no older then me ran up to one of the gunmen and whispered to him. He must have been the leader, now that Dano and Canfield were dead, because he stopped and motioned to the other gunmen to gather around him.

'What the hell's goin' on?' Gabe said.

'Beats me,' said Drifter. 'But whatever it is I don't like it.'

'Let's gun the bastards down now and get it over with,' Latigo growled.

'Easy, easy,' Liberty said. 'Let's not do anything rash.' We had reached the horses. 'We'll ride double,' she told me. Then to Latigo: 'Where's your horse?'

'Tied up in back of the cantina.'

'Go with him,' she told her father. 'Gabe and I will wait here – keep an eye on things.'

Drifter untied his horse and he and Latigo, whose jacket was leaking blood, started down the alley beside the cantina. Liberty pushed me behind her, then she and Gabe turned and kept their rifles trained on the gunmen. Despite their angry expressions, they made no attempt to close in on us.

'How're you doing?' Liberty asked Gabe, seeing

150

his blood-soaked sleeve. 'Feeling OK?'

'I'd feel a damn' sight better if I knew what those tortilla eaters were up to,' he grumbled.

'Maybe they figure it's not worth rushing us,' Liberty said. 'I mean, they know we're leaving anyway. . . .'

Drifter didn't answer, but I sensed he didn't believe that was the reason.

I heard horses and a wagon approaching. The sound was coming from the alley facing us across the street. Liberty and Gabe heard the noise too and exchanged concerned looks.

'Reinforcements?' Gabe said.

Liberty shrugged. 'It'd explain why those gunmen haven't rushed us.'

Just then I heard horses behind me. I glanced back and saw Drifter, a cigar between his teeth, and Latigo riding along the alley toward me. Liberty waited until they had joined us, then she made a stirrup with her hands and I stepped up onto the bay. Liberty mounted in front of me, then swung her horse around and motioned for the others to follow.

'What about the old man?' Drifter asked as we rode out of the alley.

'He's dead,' Liberty said, thumbing off up the street.

'We just goin' to leave him layin' there?'

'I hate it as much as you do. But under the circumstances, I think he'd forgive us.'

'What about the kid's aunt?' Latigo said.

151

Before I could tell him that she was dead too, the horses and wagon came out of the alley. They came with a rush, scattering the gunmen aside.

We all looked back. The sight we saw chilled my blood.

Mounted in the back of the wagon was a Gardner machine gun! Two men were crouched behind it, another man sat on the wagon seat handling the team.

'Jesus!' Gabe breathed.

'Better hope he's listenin',' I heard Latigo say, ' 'cause our timing stinks.'

'You an' the girl ride ahead!' Drifter shouted to Liberty. 'We'll cover you!' He swung his horse around, pulled his rifle out of its scabbard, leaped from the saddle and took cover.

Gabe and Latigo reined up on the other side of the street. Both then jumped from the saddle and dived behind some horses tied to a hitch-rail. The startled animals snorted and reared up, forcing the two men to quickly roll aside. As they did the Gardner gun opened up.

Hearing the gunfire, Liberty reined up and jerked her horse around. Clinging on to her waist, I peeked over her shoulder in time to see Latigo stop rolling and scramble back behind cover. Gabe wasn't so lucky. On the outside of Latigo, he rolled right into the line of fire. The steady hammering roar of the Gardner gun hid his cry of pain. But even as I watched the bullets chewed their way across his legs, rendering him helpless.

Seeing how badly Gabe was hurt, Latigo ignored the deadly Gardner gun and crawled painfully to his friend. 'Goddammit,' he grumbled, 'don't you know better than to lie out here in the middle of the street?'

'Shut up,' Gabe told him. 'Just shut up.'

'You know I'm gettin' real tired of savin' your sorry ass.'

Close to fainting, Gabe still tried to push Latigo back to safety. 'Get away from me, Shorty. I'd sooner bleed to death than have you help me.'

'Whine, whine, whine,' Latigo said. One-handed, he grasped Gabe's uninjured arm, struggled to his knees and tried to drag his friend to safety. But with a broken shoulder, it was a slow process.

Opposite, Drifter rested his Winchester on the wheel of the buckboard he was hiding behind and shot the man firing the Gardner gun. The big machine gun swung skyward, spraying bullets everywhere as the dead man's hand rotated the firing handle a final time. The second man crouched by the gun now jumped up and started cranking the handle again.

He aimed too low to start with and I saw the bullets kicking up the dirt in a straight line that just missed Latigo as he struggled to rescue Gabe. But immediately the man swung the Gardner gun sideways, adjusting the angle, and continued cranking the handle. My heart stopped as the second burst of bullets didn't hit the dirt at all but swept across Latigo's waist, almost cutting him in half. He froze in mid-motion, hand still clutching Gabe's arm, a mixture of agony and bewilderment on his handsome face as he realized he'd been hit. Then he slowly doubled over and crumpled to the dirt.

Behind me I heard Liberty's cry of dismay, as if someone had torn her heart out. She then swung her leg over the saddle horn, slid from the saddle and handed me the reins. 'Stay here!' she ordered. Without waiting for an answer, she pulled her rifle from its scabbard, levered in a round and strode down the center of the street toward the wagon containing the Gardner gun.

I reined in the skittish bay, bringing it under control, and sat there in the saddle watching Liberty from behind, marveling at her courage and determination to duty. She walked unwaveringly straight, lights from the cantinas casting shadows over her, making it seem like she was part of a magic-lantern show. As she walked, she pumped round after round into the man working the gun, her bullets smashing him backward, the big machine gun now silent and motionless on the jolting wagon.

Drifter saw his daughter coming. He stood up from behind the buckboard, lit a stick of dynamite from his cigar and lobbed it into the departing wagon. The explosion blew it sky-high. Flaming debris rained down, scattering the onlookers.

Liberty now drew level with her father. She didn't

stop. She didn't even turn her head to look at him. Nor do I think Drifter expected her to. He merely met her gaze, nodded to show he approved of her decision to fight and fell in beside her. I nudged the bay forward to get a closer look as they marched together down the middle of the street, rifles blazing. It was a stirring sight – a sight for the ages – a sight I knew I'd one day paint.

Shortly, they approached Gabe. Unable to get up on his bloodied legs, he saluted them; and then, from a sitting position, emptied first his rifle and then his six-gun into the dozen or so gunmen advancing along the street.

His bullets counted for at least four of them; while Liberty and her father gunned down another five. The remaining two or three gunmen turned and ran. That's when Liberty and Drifter, still side by side, dropped their spent rifles and drew their Colts, emptying them at the fleeing gunmen.

Not one survived.

It was over then.

The silence after all the gunfire was deafening.

Digging my heels into the bay I rode on until I reached Gabe, who sat alongside Latigo. He was slumped over, blood streaming from his wounds, and I jumped down and kneeled beside him.

'Gabe,' I said. 'Gabe, it's me – Hope.'

He didn't answer.

'He can't hear you,' a voice said quietly. I looked up and saw Liberty and her father standing over me.

Drifter now kneeled beside his long-time friend and gently lifted his head.

There was a warm tenderness in Drifter's eyes I'd never seen before. He leaned close and pressed his lips against Gabe's forehead. I'd never seen a man kiss another man before and yet between these two pals it seemed right and natural.

As if he'd been playing dead, Gabe suddenly opened his deep-set, uncanny, ice-blue eyes and stared, childlike, at Drifter. 'Be donkey's sono-fabitch,' he said. He grinned as if pleased with himself. Then his eyes glazed over and his head lolled back between Drifter's cupped hands.

'Is he d-dead?' I asked.

Drifter nodded. He gently laid Gabe down and closed his eyes. Then he looked across me at his daughter, who, on her knees, was cradling Latigo.

'He's gone,' she said, almost angrily. 'He's gone and I never even got to say goodbye.'

Drifter seemed to understand her pain. 'Knowin' Lefty like I do,' he said quietly, 'reckon he would've preferred it that way.'

Liberty chewed on that for a moment, then said: ' 'Least now I don't have to take him back to prison.'

'You'd've done that, would you?'

'Sounds like you're not sure I would.'

'Like to think you would.'

'So you're *not* sure?'

Drifter hesitated, as if knowing he'd stepped into trouble, and then said: 'Sure I'm sure.'

It was too late. Even at ten years old I knew that.

'Dammit,' Liberty said, flaring, 'That's so like you, Daddy!'

' 'Meanin'?'

'Acting just like every other man.'

'Now, Emily—'

'Just can't get it through your damn' head that just because I'm a woman, I can't put aside my emotions and do my duty as a lawman.'

Drifter looked at her long and hard, then, sighing, he turned to me and said: 'You heard. You think that's how I'm actin'?'

I looked at them. They were hanging on my answer. By now I loved them both and hated to disappoint either of them. So I decided to weasel out of it. 'How would I know?' I said, shrugging. 'I'm just a young'un.'

'I knew it,' Drifter began – and then he winced and screwed his eyes shut in pain.

'Oh-my-God,' Liberty said, noticing the blood trickling down his hand. 'Daddy, you're hurt!'

'Yes,' he said, sliding me a wink. 'It's my arm.'

Turned out it was just a nick. But he made the most of it – and that's how he got out of trouble.

CHAPTER TWENTY-SIX

There's not much more to tell. We buried Don Rojo outside of Palomas and covered the grave with rocks to protect him from animals. The bodies of Gabriel Moonlight, Latigo Rawlins and Aunt Connie we brought back to Santa Rosa in a tarp-covered wagon that Drifter bought at the livery stable.

By then the three of us had decided that it would be better all around if I came to live with them on their ranch outside El Paso. Of course, Liberty added, it would eventually have to be made legal by a judge; and after that, if it turned out that we all got along and were happy together, then we'd go to another judge in El Paso and sign official adoption papers.

I couldn't have been more thrilled.

But I did have a question. 'Aunt Liberty,' I said as we were crossing the border into the US, 'there's something I can't figure out.'

'What's that, scout?'

'I thought your plan to capture those two convicts was to have Latigo guard the back door of the cantina, while you, Uncle Quint and Gabe came in the front.'

'That was the plan,' she said. She glanced at her father riding beside the wagon, and though by then I was so tired I was half-asleep, I sensed she was silently scolding him.

I should have dropped the conversation then and there. I know that. But I couldn't. I mean, you only get to be ten once in a lifetime, so you have to take advantage of it.

'Then what happened?' I said. 'I mean, how come you blew up all the dynamite and gunpowder in the wagon? You must have known that would have ruined any chance of surprising them?'

'Yes,' Liberty said. She again glanced at her father, who ignored her, adding: 'I'm sure everyone who was involved did know that.'

'Well?' I said.

'It was a mistake,' Drifter said. And the way he said it made it very clear that he wanted the conversation ended.

But now Liberty couldn't let it go either. 'What my father means,' she said, enjoying herself, 'is that while he was re-lighting his cigar, the match somehow 'magically' landed in some spilled gunpowder . . . causing the wagon to explode.' She turned toward me and gave me a sly wink.

'Oh, so that's it,' I said. Despite the way I felt, I almost giggled. 'Well, like Ma use to say: "Accidents will surely happen." '